MARLENE ST ROSE was born in Trinidad and Tobago in 1945. Educated at Naparima Girls' High School and the University of the West Indies, she holds a Bachelor of Arts Degree in English and History, and a Diploma of Education. A teacher by profession, she has worked in Trinidad, Barbados and St Lucia, where she now resides.

She served as Head of the English Department at Castries Comprehensive Secondary School for seventeen years, during which time she was recruited as an Assistant Examiner for the Caribbean Examinations Council in both English A and English B marking sessions. She has also been actively involved in setting CXC examination questions, attending and assisting with workshops held in St Lucia and the region.

Following her retirement from the St Lucia Teaching Service, she was employed as a tutor in Language Arts at the Sir Arthur Lewis Community College in the Department of Continuing Studies. Presently, she is employed at a private educational institution as a tutor in English.

In December 2006, Macmillan Caribbean (UK) published the first chapter of *Into the Mosaic* in their selection of short stories entitled *The Perfume Tree*.

To Dear
Ken & Diane
with love
M St Rose
Jan. 2019

Into The Mosaic

Into The Mosaic

Marlene St Rose

ATHENA PRESS
LONDON

ISBN 10-digit: 1 84748 184 1
ISBN 13-digit: 978 1 84748 184 9

First Published 2008 by
ATHENA PRESS
Queen's House, 2 Holly Road
Twickenham TW1 4EG
United Kingdom

Printed for Athena Press

Dedicated to those who came and made a home for us

CHAPTER 1

Protect Me

Tonight, the crescent moon
Guards o'er my moonlit bed.
I, Sojourner in a foreign land
Hope and pray
That life be kind, to me
And those endeared to me –
Amidst the toil of life,
A touch to reach my outstretched
    palm
To give that calm assurance
Of a destiny
I know not now – or how –
But, hopefully is here.

G ariban Khan was a slenderly built, slightly bent woman of forty. She rose early with the break of dawn and worked busily until dusk. She was devoted to her family, her husband and their three young children. Ackbar Khan was forty-five but looked much older. He was a thoughtful, hardworking man who continually strove to improve conditions for his family; however, sometimes gruelling circumstances made life unbearable and cast him into moods of depression. Two years ago in India, he decided to leave his homeland. He was born in Lucknow, a valley region south of the Himalayas. Economic conditions had grown much worse than when he and his wife were first married. Ackbar feared for the future of his wife and his three children, whom he knew did not enjoy the best of health. Silently, he suffered the guilt of not making a better life for them and he feared that if his family's situation did not improve, disaster would ensue.

Ackbar was proud of his forefathers who had been soldiers of the Pathan caste in India, well respected for their courage and physical prowess. Ackbar's father had died when Ackbar was only six. He could remember vaguely the details of his father's face, but memories of him conjured up an unforgettable image of a tall, erect, broad-shouldered and uniformed body. His mother always spoke highly of Ackbar's father, never once regretting the life of an almost totally absent husband. As a young man, Ackbar was aware of the fact, that gradually, more provinces of India were being controlled by the British in their quest for economic power. They had established themselves as a powerful military and economic force in the country, especially in the province of Bengal. Ackbar was told that in Bengal the peasants had been complaining of harsh taxation policies imposed by the British, who had secured the right to collect revenues on behalf of the Mughul Emperor in Bengal. Eventually, when conditions became unbearable, discontent and unrest led to the Sepoy Mutiny. The sepoys, Indian soldiers, reacted violently and rebelled against the British presence. The revolt spread from Delhi to Barrackpore in Bengal where Ackbar's hometown lay in the midst of the turmoil. The mutiny tragically resulted in a brutal massacre of the sepoys, including Ackbar's father. Political stability was threatened and the *rajahs*, Indian princes, eventually surrendered power to the British.

Shortly after Ackbar and Gariban were married, his only brother died of tuberculosis and his mother wasted away through grief. Ackbar wished he could improve his financial condition, but the means of doing so were unavailable. His family inheritance had dwindled to an insignificant portion of farmland, which provided limited support. He had to secure additional means of survival. He was compelled to consider what new options he could explore.

There were rumours of Indians who travelled to the West Indies and supported themselves cultivating sugar cane on plantations, which had been deserted by recently freed slaves. It was said that the population there was scant and he simply could not imagine living in a scarcely populated area. In India, people lived in crowded settings and swarmed all over the cities, barely surviving in the most appalling conditions. Several voyages had already been made to the new lands by the British, who had transported hundreds of Indians to work on a contract basis and some of these Indians had returned after their contracts had expired. From these few, Ackbar had heard that the region consisted of several colonies, including small islands, and that the climate was very similar to that of his native land.

He pondered tediously on the issue, deliberating

whether or not he should leave his native country. He so urgently needed to make a new beginning for his children, his wife and himself. He reviewed his situation over and over again, and though he revealed his innermost thoughts to his wife, he knew that a final decision had to be made by him and soon. To surrender his ancestral way of life, to become a paid labourer and abandon the tradition of the honourable soldier's cause was to betray his heritage. But he had to believe that keeping his family alive was more important than perpetuating a dying soldier caste. He did not want his wife and children to suffer the fate of poverty and degradation. However his decision could result in dire consequences for his family in a new homeland with strange people. It was said that the poor, not only from India but from China, Europe and America, travelled to the new land in search of work and in pursuit of the quest for new opportunities in life. Traders from the East and Europeans, who had colonised those territories in the West Indies, also lived there. He could imagine a motley population of peoples thrown together in a small society. Akbar thought long and hard about his impending future and the responsibility that lay on his shoulders.

Finally, his decision was made. He would sign a five-year contract with the Indian Government to go to the West Indies as an indentured labourer. If conditions were worse than he imagined, he could always return home; if they were better, he could renew his contract or even buy a small plot of land and remain in the West Indies.

In November 1870, Ackbar, Gariban and their three

children set sail on a four-month journey to their adopted homeland, Trinidad. Aboard the sail ship, *Kanpur*, Ackbar and his family were assigned to a small, empty cabin, without any furniture provided for them. They ate and slept on the floor. Discipline and control were the order of the entire voyage. Recruits were not allowed to mingle freely. Single adult males and single adult females were quartered separately. The third group, namely families, were allowed to remain together in their family units. The largest of these three groups, by far, were single males. Single women consisted of roughly one quarter of the total number of recruits and families were an even smaller minority. All immigrants were fed twice daily. However, in spite of the rigid control exercised over the ship's passengers, a semblance of their culture was allowed in that Indian cooks prepared their meals. Sometimes, the monotony of the voyage was broken when the women were allowed to help in the kitchen and the men engaged in sweeping and scrubbing the ship. On evenings after dinner, recruits were often allowed to sit on the deck for an hour or two and be entertained by talented musicians who were among them. These musicians performed musical pieces of drumbeating and sang familiar Indian melodies.

Children were often ill on the long voyage; common ailments among them were often mumps and measles. On this particular voyage, there were two adult cases of cholera and when these patients died, their bodies were thrown overboard. Three adult cases of malaria were treated by Indian nurses in the ship's hospital and fortunately survived. The long voyage was interrupted by a single stop at Durban in the Cape of

Good Hope, to purchase coal and provisions before crossing the Atlantic Ocean. One night, when the ship was scheduled to leave port for its onward journey, the weather worsened suddenly. The ship's occupants were fearful that the captain might set sail despite the inclement weather, but fortunately he was advised by the port manager to remain in harbour because of the existing wind turbulence and rough seas. The *Kanpur* was forced to dock for two days at Durban, after which time the voyage proceeded safely.

Ackbar, Gariban and especially their children, were anxious for their journey to come to an end. On approaching their intended destination they were informed that, before disembarking at the Port of Spain harbour, all recruits had first to be taken to Nelson Island, where medical personnel needed to check them for diseases and ailments with which they might be afflicted. If necessary, the sick recruits would be detained on Nelson Island until they recovered. Only healthy individuals would be allowed to re-board the ship and sail on to Port of Spain. Fortunately Ackbar, Gariban and their three children were given a clean bill of health.

When the ship finally docked at Port of Spain, the siren shrilled a loud, piercing whistle. The waiting immigrants shuffled along the deck, clutching their precious bundles and some huddling together in family groups. A turbaned official eased his way past them to the top of the gangway.

'Hurry, hurry; keep your women and children together!' he shouted in Hindustani, as he led the procession. Beneath them, on the platform alongside the docks, stood a number of white men dressed in white shirts and khaki breeches, wearing white rounded hats and tall, black, rubber boots.

One of them stepped forward and asked the Indian official, 'How many are there on this trip?'

'Two hundred and eighty-six, Sahib,' the turbaned official replied.

'Can they speak English?' he probed.

'No, Sahib, but they may understand a little,' was the reply.

'Read the list quickly; I've been here for the past two hours. I'm here to collect a family of five: father, mother, two boys and a girl, should be quite an investment. One Ackbar Khan,' he said impatiently.

Ackbar's family was assigned to Mr Dickinson's cocoa plantation. Mother, father and children boarded the wagon, driven by the planter's handyman, Lal. The horses galloped through the empty streets of Port of Spain, through Maraval, past the homes of the wealthy city folk, and towards the heights of Maracas.

The hills rose majestically in the distance. The air was cool and refreshing, clean, healthy and pure. Nature was alive and abundant. Birds hovered in the air; flowers blossomed and fruit hung heavy from mature trees. The awesome profusion of colour and lushness welcomed the newcomers. The morning mist had cleared and the pink-grey hues of dawn dissipated. Tropical warmth greeted the strangers. The grandeur of immortelles speckled with yellow and red, shaded bursting yellow cocoa pods and red-berried coffee shrubs. Red clay banks embraced a gushing river amidst the moss-green silhouette of fertility. Maracas appeared to be a valley of natural profusion. To Ackbar, this was a promising new beginning, a second chance in life to build a new home in a world far from his native land.

Within one week of her family's arrival in Maracas, Gariban transformed the appearance of their small, neglected, carat-roofed dwelling. The frame of the two-roomed structure was wooden, but its walls were made of clay and were supported by a framework of twigs and grass. Unsightly gaping holes, like deep sockets, allowed rays of sunlight into the rooms. Gariban began to collect the materials needed to repair the walls. Her neighbours, who were also occupants of barracks and indentured labourers like Ackbar, were helpful in advising her where in the valley she would acquire clay easily. While Ackbar worked in the cocoa fields, Gariban and her three small children fetched and carried red Maracas clay, twigs and tall grasses to repair their hut. With that task completed, Gariban began to prepare a plot of land behind the barracks to grow vegetables. She decided to grow Ackbar's favourite vegetables – string beans, pumpkins and *baigan*. In the near future, she planned to build a small fowl coop and begin rearing a few chickens.

One evening, a few weeks after their arrival in their new homeland, Gariban was cleaning her makeshift kitchen on the tiny porch when she was surprised by an unusual visitor, whose galloping horse raced down the path leading to the small hut.

'Dat mus' be de Reverend!' shouted Indrani, the eldest child. She spoke in Hindustani, a dialect of Hindi, as was their custom among family members in the absence of strangers. 'Quiet!' cautioned Gariban. 'Let yuh brudder go to see.'

'Who coming, Bhai?' she asked her elder son. Although Indrani was the eldest child, her brother, one year her junior was expected to greet any visitor to the house, especially strangers and males. Among East Indians, women and girls were forbidden to be familiar with strangers. Sanwar peered through the opening in the wall, his unkempt head of hair barely reaching above the wooden window sill. He perched his chin on the rough, uneven piece of wood that steadied the framework of the window. Hurrying to his mother's side, and holding on to her skirt with one hand and brushing it gently with the other hand, he said, 'Is de Reverend on de horse, Mai! What to say?'

'Tell him Baap in de garden. He not coming back before dark,' she answered abruptly.

Sanwar rushed out of the carat-roofed house and hurried towards the front yard where Reverend James Thompson sat on his horse, waiting.

'Good afternoon, Reverend. Mai say to tell yuh dat Baap not coming back until – before dark.'

'I don't want to see your father, son. I would just like to invite the whole family to a special service on Sunday at the school. Tell your mother, all the children and your father that they can come at nine o'clock in the morning.'

'Yes, Sahib,' replied Sanwar, whose manner was respectful but awkward for a child of only eight.

After this brief conversation, Sanwar relayed the missionary's message to his family. The other two children seemed excited, but his mother became pensive. Her neighbours had warned her about an impending visit by the stranger, but she did not think it would have occurred so soon. She was compelled to think over this new situation, which she faced suddenly. This is a strange world, she thought, why do they want us to change our ways of Allah? Gariban was worried; her husband would never approve of the Reverend's persuasive devices to make converts of their children.

On his return home, Gariban spared her husband a night of anxiety, which the missionary's message threatened. She decided she would tell him about the invitation early the next morning, before the children awoke. Sanwar rose early too, but he was not a precocious child and understood the importance of the privacy that existed between his parents and among adults in general. At the break of dawn, Gariban lit her fire with small pieces of dry sticks within a *chulha*, an enclosed fireplace. It was an oval formation of red clay, about twelve inches high and smoothly moulded. She applied a new layer of red clay weekly to restore a clean, smooth surface. Upon this invention, she placed her pot, which had a permanently darkened bottom. Once a week, she scrubbed her priceless utensils with ashes, a detergent that worked wonders on heavy metal. She grated a cocoa stick to make a hot beverage for breakfast and baked flat round *rotis*, which she tossed onto her *tawa* or baking stone, grilling the dough to a rich brown on each side. Ackbar entered the small room silently and sat on a low stool facing the open doorway.

'De Reverend invite we to a service tomorrow

morning,' Gariban informed him. Without looking up, she waited for his response.

'I prefer to have meh own prayers here,' replied Ackbar. 'Sometimes yuh never know what de Reverend telling you or yuh children. I dohn want him to t'ink dat we ungrateful, but if we want to worship Allah dat is we business. Maybe de Reverend could help we get a horse instead of giving we a new god.'

Gariban was pleased with this reply, but said nothing; her silence supported his opinion. Her two younger children might be disappointed. Manwar and Indrani were anxious for the opportunity to meet other children, but there was more than enough for them to do at home.

However, Ackbar did not want to offend the missionary, who seemed to have a special fondness for his elder son, Sanwar. At first, he allowed his children to attend Sunday school at the Christian church and then thought he had made a wrong decision. Sanwar requested if he could help the Reverend feed his horses and clean the animal stable. He seemed to enjoy looking after the animals; after all, horses were an integral part of everyday life in India and probably reminded him of home. The missionary allowed Sanwar to groom his two horses and paid him a shilling every Saturday, which he promptly gave to his father on his return home. Sanwar worked conscientiously and was proud of his small earnings.

Gariban observed him carefully, but she could not fathom the depth of his thoughts. She discerned in him a tendency to be attracted to the unfamiliar practices of strangers in this unfamiliar world, their new homeland. He was a polite, well-behaved son, but was prone to spells of lonely silence, when he would sit on the front step with his chin cupped in both hands, his wide-eyed stare delving deeply into the unknown. He was not a chatty, lively, bursting-with-energy child like her two other children. He was so different and strange at times.

'I hope he go have a good future; on de odder hand I hope he is not a dreamer,' she murmured to herself.

In spite of the pride and nostalgia he felt for his native India, Ackbar was grateful for the small mercies which his new homeland offered him. At first, it was humiliating for him to work as a peasant from morning to evening in the unbearable heat of the plantation; but after five years, he hoped he would be able to improve his situation and purchase a small plot of land. With luck, he could still be employed on the cocoa estate. His overseer was a familiar sight who insisted on 'a fair day's work for a fair day's pay,' but Ackbar earned more than an honest wage. Many plantations were abandoned after the Abolition of Slavery Act of 1833 and this one, on which he worked, employed a number of varied labourers. It was difficult to find labourers to work in the hilly areas like Maracas and usually indentured Indians were assigned to them.

However, conditions on the cocoa estates were not as gruelling as on larger sugar estates and for that advantage, Ackbar was grateful. There were several Indians like himself whom he saw only at work; they were not allowed to communicate at length except during the midday break. He knew some of their names, but did not understand their dialects because they came from different regions of India. Some Indian women also worked on the same plantation as he did. Like him, they were responsible for providing their own food. On this island, he understood, labourers were well paid and workers from other islands came to Trinidad seeking higher wages. Labour was scarce and it was believed that much larger numbers of Indians would be brought to the island But, Ackbar was prepared to accept conditions as they were for the time being.

The small plot of land which was allocated to him would provide the food his family needed. His two sons, Sanwar, aged eight, and Manwar, aged six, helped in the vegetable garden while he worked on the plantation during the day. The boys were young but industrious. They knew what was expected of them. Some indentured labourers brought their sons to work with them, but he did not. They were better off at home growing food for the family and helping their mother. On Saturday afternoons, he spent time with his family and on Sundays, he and the boys worked in the small garden. They helped to remove the weeds, water the plants and secure the bean vines while he did the more difficult chores.

His five-year contract would soon come to an end and he had decided to remain in Trinidad, at least, temporarily. At the inception of Indian indentured labour, after completing a five-year contract an Indian immigrant was entitled to a return fare home but the British Government now claimed it could no longer afford such a practice. The labourers who wished to return to India had to pay their own return fares.

Ackbar discovered he could renew his contract annually after the initial contract and hoped that conditions for released indentures would improve in the near future.

He felt he was at a grave disadvantage living in the north of the island. Maracas village was an isolated area that hindered easy movement to surrounding areas. He heard from workers on the cocoa plantation that other parts of the island were being developed and there was even a mosque built by Muslims recently in the South. His was the only Muslim family in Maracas and he longed to enjoy the brotherhood of worship among people of his own religion. While the white planters and the government acknowledged the Christian religions, all Indians were considered pagans and neither their marriages nor their children were legitimate. Ackbar felt excluded from a communal life that he had so deeply cherished in his homeland and felt profoundly homesick.

One Saturday, Sanwar left home early to groom the missionary's horses. When he returned, his face was beaming. Ackbar had retired indoors earlier than expected because he had felt ill while working in the garden. Sanwar was happy to see his father inside their hut so early, but Gariban was alarmed. Although, her husband did not complain, she knew he was not as strong as he was when they had first arrived in Trinidad. Tiresome work on the plantation had taken its toll on his body. As Ackbar relaxed in their hammock, Sanwar entered the room.

'Baap,' he greeted his father as he gave him his one-shilling wage. 'I want to ask you somet'ing, Baap.'

'Yes?' replied Ackbar, impressed by the boy's seriousness.

'Reverend Thompson say I is a good worker and he want to teach me at school. He say if I learn well he could find a work for me.'

'Where de school?' asked Ackbar.

'A five-mile walk to Tunapuna,' replied Sanwar.

'Every day?' asked Ackbar.

'Every day, from Monday to Friday,' said his son.

'An' church on Sunday too?' queried Ackbar.

'I dohn know, Baap,' replied the boy innocently.

Ackbar saw through this move, but said no more. He could sense that his older son was impressed by something in the white man's way of life, but could not say exactly what it was. Sanwar was attracted to people who were strange to him, and about whom he knew very little. In India people were very wary about the white man. There, the British always held important positions; they were wealthy and powerful, and caused a great deal of suffering among the Indians. Ackbar was uncertain if the Reverend wanted to use his son or help him. He knew that Sanwar was an intelligent boy and could not deny him the opportunity for success. Ackbar had been stunned for a moment, but not shocked. His intuition warned him to be prepared for surprises. He would allow the boy to attend school, but would observe developments very carefully.

That night, Ackbar and Gariban shared each other's fears of their son being influenced by a new culture. When they had first left India for Trinidad, they had not envisaged that they would meet missionaries who would pose a threat to their family. The plantation owners had no objections to the missionaries' quest to convert all Indians. Why was it imperative that they impose their religion on other people's beliefs and why were they so determined to poison the Indians' minds against their tradition? What made the English God superior to Allah? It seemed that, as Indians, they were facing a mighty force against which they had no resistance.

Although Ackbar had given Sanwar permission to attend school, he was not prepared to sit back and allow others to usurp control of his son's mind. He decided that as soon as his second annual labour contract came to an end, he would sell his small hut and garden, and move to another part of the island – to an area where Muslims practised their own religion. Allah would never forgive him for casting his people's sacred beliefs aside. Furthermore, he longed to worship with his brothers in a mosque, the holy place of Allah.

Sanwar rose early every morning to help his father with miscellaneous chores around the house before going to school. He felt guilty about not being able to help every day in the vegetable garden, but he tended the animals whenever he was at home. Also, on Saturdays, he often went to St Joseph to make a meagre purchase of items that his mother needed.

Sanwar enjoyed each day he spent at school and learned a bit of English from his association with Reverend Thompson. Sometimes, he attempted to converse with the children at school. In his class, there were ten children altogether. Besides himself, there were three other Indian children; they spoke Hindi, a language Sanwar did not fully understand. Their father owned a small store in St Joseph and sold kitchen utensils mainly. He thought of his mother and was sure she would have loved to own some of those items: enamel bowls, shining metal pots and pans, long-handled spoons and sharp knives. Three other children in the class were of mixed ethnic background – mulattoes – and the Reverend's three children completed the group. At first, Sanwar felt very odd; he was singular in many respects. He was beginning a new experience which he didn't understand clearly, but to which he looked forward.

One day, Reverend Thompson introduced a young man of about twenty-four to the class. Mr Gill was a Canadian who would be responsible for teaching the children English and Arithmetic. Reverend Thompson would instruct them in Religious Knowledge. Sanwar knew how his father felt about his involvement in the new religion, so he decided not to utter a word about Christianity when he returned home.

Even though he was not the oldest student in his class, Sanwar was by far the most alert and made such quick progress that he was commended by Mr Gill. However, he was reluctant to relate the details of his daily experiences at school to his family for fear that his father would prohibit him from attending the classes that he enjoyed. When they did enquire about his activities at school, his answers were usually brief. He was not eager to repeat what he learnt about the new religion and the beliefs taught about Christianity. This would greatly offend his father. He was by nature a sensitive and an unassuming boy, and also did not want his brother and sister to be displeased by his enthusiasm since they did not have the opportunity to attend school. Now that he was unavailable to help at home during the week, his brother Manwar performed the task of cultivating most of the vegetables the family consumed. He also helped to tend their two cows, goats and chickens. While Manwar enjoyed his responsibility, he sometimes became tired and restless. Sanwar hoped that his continuous absence from home would not arouse the jealousy of his young brother.

One Friday afternoon, Reverend Thompson asked Mr Gill to send Sanwar to him before he left for home. Sanwar was surprised. He had never been to the Reverend's house. Maybe, he thought, the Reverend wished to extend another invitation to his family to attend Sunday service. Sanwar did as he was told and as he approached the house, he spotted Reverend Thompson seated on the veranda, with one leg extended high on a chair. Sanwar proceeded slowly.

'Come on up, Khan,' he called, 'I have an important assignment for you. I would like a responsible person to deliver a message for me to Reverend Hall in San Fernando.' Sanwar was stunned. Surely, Reverend Thompson could find someone else to deliver this message, he thought.

'I'm sorry, Sir. I dohn know San Fernando,' Sanwar apologised.

'Oh, don't worry,' assured the Minister. 'Transportation will be provided. Carl will take you to the train station in the wagon. I will buy you two train tickets, one for the trip to San Fernando and another for the return trip. Reverend Hall is expecting me on that train, but I've injured my leg and cannot travel tomorrow. I shall write a letter to him and explain. Besides, this is an excellent opportunity for you to see another part of the island.'

Sanwar was speechless. He did not have the opportunity to refuse Reverend Thompson's request, nor did he have the audacity to reject the confidence which had been placed in him. He felt honoured and hoped that his father would not object to the Reverend's request.

Ackbar did not object to his son's eagerly awaited adventure. He did not want to deny him a chance to learn more about the island. The journey would allow his son to see the south of the island, and possibly meet young men his own age and make friends. He couldn't deny him this trip. Sanwar was a brave boy and seemed eager to see and understand more about this new society. At five o'clock on Saturday morning, Carl arrived to take Sanwar to the train station in Port of Spain. Gariban gave him a small parcel of sandwiched bakes for breakfast on his long journey. Carl handed him two tickets and said that he would be waiting for him at the train station at six o'clock that same evening.

'De Reverend like yuh Sanwar,' said Carl, as he waved goodbye to him. 'Enjoy de long drive and be careful.' Carl was fourteen years old. He was the son of a former slave. His father had died and he was the eldest child in his family. His mother worked as a kitchen maid for Reverend Thompson. Carl spoke a language which was basically broken English – 'a

Creole dialect,' as Mr Gill called it. Whenever he spoke, Carl aided verbal communication with a multitude of gestures and facial expressions. An arduous worker, he was indispensable to the Thompsons.

At the train station in Port of Spain, Sanwar boarded one of the small carriages which consisted of twelve wooden, stationary benches. They were arranged in pairs, each one facing the other. There were six pairs of benches, three on either side of a narrow aisle. Sanwar was the only occupant of the carriage when the train started its long journey; but he was joined by a family of eight, who boarded the train at Carapichaima, one of the fourteen stations at which the train stopped before its journey ended in San Fernando. When Sanwar arrived at his destination, he was surprised to see the number of people who had travelled in the other carriages – a motley crowd of different ethnic backgrounds.

Many wagons were waiting in the station yard to transport the arriving friends and relatives. He was confused at first, not knowing in which direction to look for Reverend Hall, when an East Indian boy, no taller than himself, approached him and said, 'Who you looking for?'

'I have a message for Reverend Hall from de Reverend in St Joseph. You know him?'

'I know him,' replied the boy and pointed to a white man seated in a wagon. Sanwar observed that the gentleman was becoming impatient as he glared through the crowd of moving people. He quickly walked up to the wagon and addressed the white stranger, 'Good morning, Sir. I would like to introduce myself on behalf of Reverend Thompson. He was unable to travel because of an injured leg.'

'And who are you?' asked the white stranger.

'My name is Sanwar Khan and I attend Reverend Thompson's school in Tunapuna. Reverend Thompson asked me to deliver this letter to you, Sir.'

Sanwar gave the letter to the stranger who watched him curiously. He waited silently while the letter was being read. Reverend Hall nodded while he raced through the long letter. Then he raised his head. He seemed a little disappointed that his friend had not arrived, then soon realised it was his turn to respond to the waiting boy.

'Come aboard the wagon. What did you say your name was?' he asked.

'Sanwar Khan, Sir. I have to return home today, Sir. I have a little time before I catch the next train to Port of Spain.'

'There's no need to worry about that, Khan,' was the reply. 'You cannot wait here until two o'clock. It is only eleven o'clock and the train does not leave until two. I'm sure you must be famished. You'll have something to eat then Boodoo will bring you back to the station.'

'Thank you, Sir,' said Sanwar, as he quickly stepped into the wagon. Within ten minutes, they arrived at Reverend Hall's house.

While Reverend Hall wrote a letter for Sanwar to take to St Joseph, Sanwar decided to stroll around the yard for a while. Boodoo, Reverend Hall's messenger-cum-wagon-driver-cum-handyman accompanied him and kept him well informed during their short walk.

'What's the name of this place?' enquired Sanwar.

'Victoria Village,' answered Boodoo sharply. 'Dis is de first time yuh come here?' Without waiting for an answer, he continued, 'Me Mai and Baap die in de cane field in a fire over dere.' He pointed towards the south-east, 'so de Reverend tell me to come and work for him. He good to me, to de children at school and to all de people in de big village. Next time, when yuh come back I go drive yuh to de big village.'

'What's the name of the village?' asked Sanwar, his curiosity aroused.

'Mission Village,' replied Boodoo.

'Many children go to school there?' inquired Sanwar.

'Plenty, plenty children! It have school, church and plenty houses. Next Saturday, de Church having a bazaar wit' games and singing and plenty t'ings to eat. Yuh Reverend sure to come; he like t'ings dere. I always drive him to de big village.' Boodoo was excited about the forthcoming events.

Reverend Hall appeared on the top of the stairs. He quickly descended and walked towards the wagon. Boodoo and Sanwar followed him. Boodoo drove to the train station. Reverend Hall gave Sanwar a letter for Reverend Thompson and wished him a pleasant journey. Sanwar thanked him for his hospitality, waved goodbye to Boodoo and boarded his train – little was he aware of the contents of the letter which he carried. He had impressed Reverend Hall, who had written to his friend:

Dear Edward,

I have not before now, encountered in Trinidad a young East Indian so well spoken in our language and respectful in manner, as your student, Khan. He is very young and may benefit a great deal from our school. We need intelligent young converts to continue our work in the Church. We are also in great need of teachers to expand the school. We may discuss the issue further when we meet next Saturday to celebrate our Harvest. I will expect you at the train station at ten, or thereabouts. May God give you a speedy recovery and ensure you have a safe journey.

Until we meet,

Sincerely,

William Hall.

During the following week, Sanwar's enthusiasm wore off as he settled down to the routine of attending school and assisting Reverend Thompson when he needed help. One afternoon before classes had ended; he was surprised to see his brother rush into the classroom gesticulating frantically before Mr Gill. He left his seat hurriedly and approached them.

'What happen, Beta? What yuh doing here?' he asked.

'Bhai!' blurted out the distraught child. 'Yuh have to come quick. Mai gone to hospital wit' Baap. A big immortelle tree fall on him in de cocoa field, and Mai say he not talking or moving.'

Overcome with fear and anxiety, Manwar began to cry. Between sobs, he was able to relay his mother's request to his brother, stammering as he relayed the urgent message, 'Mai say to ask de Reverend if he could help, get a doctor to see Baap – and to come quick.'

The suddenness of the event stunned Mr Gill. He realised that the boys were caught in a tragic situation and appreciated the urgency of their mother's request. Sanwar was overcome by the enormity of his responsibility and was fully aware that no time should be wasted in the task assigned to him.

'Please, Sir,' he moaned. 'I must leave now to ask the Reverend for help.'

'Of course, Khan, hurry on. I wish your father a quick recovery,' he uttered. His words fell on deaf ears as the brothers made a hasty exit. The students' stares followed the two boys' movements until they were out of sight.

The brothers approached Reverend Thompson's house, which was adjacent to the school, and were told to wait at the foot of the stairs by the housekeeper. Sanwar explained his father's dilemma to the Minister and repeated his mother's request. Reverend Thompson summoned Carl immediately and the foursome made a hasty departure for St Joseph hospital. When they arrived, they met Gariban kneeling at Ackbar's bedside, waiting for a sign of recognition from her injured husband. Reverend Thompson and Carl left the family members to console each other. Eventually, Sanwar and his brother returned home to stay with their sister, who had been left alone all evening while Gariban spent the night at her husband's side.

Unaware of her presence, Ackbar's body lay heavy and limp on the small bed. His face was swollen and his complexion blotchy and darkened. The next morning when she awoke from her sleepy vigil in a corner of the room, Gariban collapsed on seeing her husband's body completely shrouded in a white cloth tucked in beneath the mattress. Sanwar and his brother returned to the hospital before dawn and were horrified to learn of their father's death. Silently, they knelt at Ackbar's bedside while Gariban, overcome with confused grief, clung to her husband's rigid body.

Ackbar was laid to rest beneath the shade of a huge flamboyant tree in a small cemetery for labourers at the Maracas foothills. The workers prepared a burial place for Ackbar while Mr Dickinson looked on silently as Ackbar's shrouded figure was lowered to his final resting place. A light drizzle showered the mourners beneath the umbrella spread of red flamboyant blossoms. Manwar and Indrani wept continuously, comforting each other in their sorrow. Gariban, bereaved and helpless, stared blankly as Sanwar and Carl helped to shovel red dirt onto the mound that marked Ackbar's breathless repose. Reverend Thompson prayed and sang, and Sanwar and Carl repeated a seemingly familiar prayer, the Family Prayer. But these were all empty words to her; they meant nothing.

That night, the crescent moon appeared. Gariban remained under the flamboyant tree, praying on her hands and knees and begging Allah to guide and protect her husband in the new world to which he had departed. She knew that Ackbar's greatest wish had been to return to India and to worship among his own people, but that wish was now lost for ever. He had surrendered his heritage; he had forsaken his homeland and his people to give them a better life, and now he had sacrificed his own life in what seemed to be a wasted effort. He had been a good man – honest and courageous, kind and patient, a dutiful husband and father, and a hard worker, determined to succeed at all costs, yet humble in the presence of Allah.

It was ten o'clock that night when Sanwar decided he should lead his mother away from his father's grave and encourage her to go to bed. He led her slowly into the house, to the table, and gave her a cup of tea which she sipped. She sat as though in a dream, not quite believing what was happening. No one spoke, each heartbroken child fearing a renewed outburst of her grief. Sanwar persuaded his sister, Indrani, to retire for the night while he and Manwar sat on the front step in the faint glow of the moonlight.

'What we going to do now, Bhai?' asked the distraught boy, his eyes swollen and tear-filled.

'You and me have to decide dat, Beta. Mai in no condition to talk about anyt'ing so we must decide. I have to stay home and help wit' de garden so at least we could have enough food,' he insisted.

'And what about yuh school?' interrupted the young boy.

'That can wait,' replied Sanwar, 'you and Baap work too hard in de garden to leave it now.'

'De garden go give us food, Bhai, but what about

money to buy t'ings dat Mai want?' asked the worried boy.

'I was t'inking we could sell some food in de market on Saturdays,' suggested Sanwar. 'You t'ink you will like dat?'

'I will like dat,' beamed Manwar. 'I like to sell in de market and bring home de money for Mai.'

'Good,' replied Sanwar. 'Maybe I can ask Reverend Thompson to help us by getting some of his friends to buy vegetables every Saturday.'

Sanwar's brother was in deep thought as he gazed into the hazy distance before him. Sanwar was about to touch him on his shoulder to gain his attention when he blurted out, 'But Bhai, yuh could get Baap work on de cocoa plantation! Since Baap gone, de boss mus' want a man to do dat work. I could see about de garden by mehself.'

Sanwar was startled by this unexpected suggestion. For a few seconds, he was silent; but, he quickly and almost falteringly answered his brother, 'Oh no, Beta, dat is too much for you to do. You can't manage dat. I will help you.'

After his brother went to bed that night, Sanwar thought of his family's problems, the most immediate being earning a steady income. The only solution seemed to be concentrating on the family garden, which his brother looked after so diligently. He avoided any consideration that his mother or Indrani should seek employment on the cocoa plantation. His father would never have entertained such an idea. He was sure he could replace his father on the plantation, but he hated the thought of working in the fields. He had seen East

Indians mocked and humiliated because they did slaves' work. There were stories of severe punishment meted out to indentured workers by plantation supervisors because they had left their dwellings without their identification passes. These were documents issued to all East Indian labourers by the authorities and only entitled them to very limited movement. They were not allowed to enter the towns; their movements were confined to a small radius around the plantations where they worked. Their situation was not much different from that of the recently freed slaves, and they could face imprisonment and be left to the mercy of the legal system if they broke the rules. Sanwar felt he could not endure such humiliation. He was fully aware of the deprived status of his family. Now, with the loss of his father they were without his protection as well. As the elder son of the family, he was forced to assume the roles of protector and bread-winner.

At that moment, he came face to face with the enormity of these responsibilities for the first time since his father's death. For the time being, he would assume the role of a farmer. He would have liked to continue attending school; he knew that there was so much to be discovered in those books which Mr Gill had showed the students. One day, he would pursue it – this was his dream. He rose wearily from the step like an old man. The sky was lost in a blue-black hue of darkness that engulfed the entire world around him – his father's world. 'May Allah bless you and protect you, Baap,' he uttered prayerfully.

Sanwar was missed at school, but Mr Gill assumed that his student needed time to recover from his father's sudden death. It was Gariban, however, who struggled with recovering from her husband's death. The shock of her husband's passing left an emptiness within her and compelled her to retreat into silence and disbelief, often in the privacy of her room. Sanwar realised his mother would be unable to cope with the daily pressures of life for a long time. He observed that she lost concentration quickly, even in everyday household chores which she had once mastered with such efficiency. It was difficult to converse with her and avoid the memory of his dear father.

Most of the household chores fell on Indrani's shoulders. Ackbar's death made Gariban helpless but imposed a responsibility on her daughter, which the young girl did not refuse. Indrani was a source of comfort to her mother and the backbone of all household activity. She had learned to perform almost every household chore under the guidance of her mother; now, she used her own intelligence to organise a daily routine. She became the new nerve centre of the home. Although two years Sanwar's senior, Indrani did not attempt to question his plans. She had a confidence in him, which no other member of the family shared. As far as she was concerned, he was her big brother. She knew that he was an intelligent boy and now, that he had the responsibility of guiding them into the future, it was her duty to give him all the support he needed.

One week after his father's death, Sanwar decided to visit Reverend Thompson. As he walked along the muddy five-mile track that led to the Minister's house, he wondered if his plans for the immediate future were feasible. He knew very little about farming and budgeting, but his brother, Manwar, had learnt a great deal from his father. He hoped they would make a prosperous team with some help from the Reverend. His family's survival depended on their success. The children had been dismissed from school only a short while before Sanwar arrived in the school yard. He was greeted by Mr Gill, who was pleased to see him.

'How are you, Sanwar?' he asked.

'I am well, Sir. Do you know where the Reverend is? Can I see him, Sir? I want to ask him a favour,' Sanwar said, with a sense of urgency.

'He's inside. He came to the school this morning, but remained indoors this afternoon. I need to speak to him myself. Come with me, I'll let him know you're here.'

Mr Gill ascended the stairs while Sanwar waited below. One minute later, Reverend Thompson appeared on the veranda. Looking down at Sanwar standing in the yard at the bottom of the stairs, he called, 'Come on up, my boy. I've been wondering about you. How is your mother?'

'Mai is not well these days, Sir. She is saying very little to us,' he answered.

'Very withdrawn, eh? She'll get over it soon. And what about you – when will you be back at school?' He seemed concerned.

'I cannot come back to school yet, Sir. I must help my brother in the garden; he is too small to manage on his own. I wonder, Sir...'

'Yes, my boy?'

'I wonder if you can help us, Sir.' His voice was pleading.

'Of course, of course, in any way I can. How would you like me to help?' the Reverend asked.

'Sir,' Sanwar began shyly. 'My brother and I are thinking of selling some of our vegetables at the market on Saturday. We never did this before and are afraid that we might fail in our plan. You could help us a great deal, Sir, if you ask some of your friends to buy from us.'

Reverend Thompson had not expected this kind of request. The frown on his face revealed surprise. He replied as if explaining the problem to himself. 'Oh, I understand! You would like me to help you find dependable, weekly customers, a guaranteed market for your produce. You are an adventurous chap, my boy! I'll do my best. Bring along your family to service on Sunday and we'll advertise your enterprise. I'm sure you and your brother will be successful,' he assured the young boy.

'Thank you, Sir,' replied Sanwar, as he bowed his head in gratitude. He turned around and retraced his steps down the stairs.

As he walked home, Sanwar was deep in thought. He appreciated the Reverend's interest in his plans, and he hoped and prayed they would be successful. He knew that he and Manwar would have to work very hard to make their plans materialise. He knew there would be problems to face in this new venture. He would try to discuss the issue with his mother; maybe she could offer some advice.

It was almost dinner time when Sanwar arrived home. He was pleasantly surprised to see his mother helping Indrani in the kitchen. They were singing an

Indian song which told the story of a young soldier, who left his wife and child behind when he went to battle. On his return home he discovered that his house was deserted, and his wife and child had gone to live elsewhere. In his search for them, he stopped at a house to ask for some water. He was invited in and given some food by a servant girl, whom he recognised as his wife. The song ended with clapping of hands and a swirling dance that brought Indrani face to face with Sanwar's entry into the kitchen. When she felt her head stop reeling, she blurted out, 'Bhai? What de Reverend say?'

'He promise to help us,' replied her brother.

'But yuh must come to service on Sunday,' Gariban interrupted.

'Yes, Mai; it important dat he help us. So I have to go. He has many friends, Mai, and he will tell others to buy from us.'

'But at de loss of yuh religion, meh son. Allah forgive yuh, meh son, for trading yuh religion for a few coins,' she pleaded.

'We need de money, Mai. We not begging de Reverend for food or money – he just helping us to get some people to buy t'ings we carry to de market on Saturday,' he tried to explain.

'Son, how yuh going to carry dat food to de market? All yuh boys too small to walk wit' all dat.' She thought the task was impossible for her sons. Sanwar was silent. He had not thought of this problem.

'We go make a box-cart,' interjected Manwar, 'we jus' have to buy some nails and a wheel. We have plenty old wood in de shed, Mai!'

'And push dat for four miles?' asked Indrani.

'De cart is a good idea,' pronounced Sanwar. 'And it cheap too. Tomorrow we can buy de nails and a wheel and start working on it. Mai, don't worry; we just trying to make a few shillings every Saturday,' he said to her.

Gariban admired her elder son's courage and determination. He was only fourteen and yet possessed the mind of a man. Since his father's death, she had not once seen him depressed or annoyed. He had accepted the responsibility which fell on his shoulders and she marvelled at his ability to seek help among strangers. She had to admit that he was a practical person by nature, though so young. The small family savings which her husband had accumulated should not be used indiscriminately. They needed money to buy items at the shop. Ackbar's six shillings a week meant a great deal to the family; they needed to earn just as much. Sanwar was right. He had more foresight than she had thought him capable of having. She only wished she could be of some help. To think she was dependent on her fourteen year old son was painful enough.

The next Sunday, Sanwar and his brother attended a service at the school. Gariban refused to be persuaded into accompanying her children to a Christian service. In her mind, Christians had no respect for other people's religion. She was annoyed that her children had to be subjected to the influence of strangers and their beliefs. If Ackbar was alive, he would be able to change the course of their lives. If only there was a Mosque nearby where she could take all the children to worship. This would make her so happy and would satisfy the lifelong wish of her dear husband.

Indrani stayed at home with her mother while the boys left for Tunapuna. Gariban drowned her sorrows by repeating a Muslim prayer, which she and Ackbar had often said together at dawn. Although Ackbar owned a copy of the Holy Qur'an, it was of no use to her. She could not read. She could only repeat those prayers which she had learned through constant repetition as Ackbar had read them aloud. He had been her guide, not only in the material world but in the spiritual one as well. Twice daily they had prayed together – at dawn and at night, before retiring to bed. He had been the only person in the whole world in whom she had such great confidence. Her life had depended on him and now he had gone, and left her and her children at the mercy of a strange land. She was lonely, lost and desperate. She didn't know how to survive without him; she didn't know if she could survive without him.

Reverend Thompson was jubilant at the service. The crowd consisted largely of children between the ages of five to twelve, a smaller number of teenage girls and four adults. Most of them were like Sanwar, children of East Indian indentured labourers. Many of them were from the Tunapuna orphanage, which accommodated the children of contracted labourers who had died during their term of employment or on their sea voyage to Trinidad. Reverend Thompson's family and Mr Gill were the only white members of the congregation. While the Reverend read a Bible passage about Jesus and His raising the dead to life,

x

Sanwar thought of the prospects that lay ahead for his market enterprise. After the hour-long service – which took the form more of a Sunday school than of an adult service – Mr Ram, a former Hindu believer and the only adult convert in the congregation, distributed pamphlets to the children. On these, were printed pictures of Jesus preaching to the Jews. There was a Bible passage that corresponded to the picture story as well as a prayer and suggested reading from the Bible. All this was written in English. Mr Ram worked as a part-time bookkeeper in a hardware store in Port of Spain and was fluent in both English and Hindi. Although a Hindu by birth, he had worked for a long time among his English-speaking employers. He was invaluable to the Canadian missionary, whose ardent desire was to convert the Indian community to Christianity and, when the time came, educate them in a culture alien to them. Mr Ram was the interpreter and counsellor to the missionary in his work among the Indian population around St Joseph. On Saturday afternoons and Sundays, he stayed with the Thompsons, and after Sunday school he chatted with the children.

To Sanwar, it seemed that the Reverend had forgotten all about him and his request, which he had made almost a week ago. While his brother, Manwar, mingled with the children, reminding himself of childhood pleasures, Sanwar waited for the opportunity to speak privately with Reverend Thompson.

Mr Ram began to address the children in Hindi, while Sanwar, unnoticed by most, approached the

Reverend, who was absorbed in a Bible passage he was reading.

'Excuse me, Sir, I...'

'Oh!' remarked the Reverend, surprised to see Sanwar appear so suddenly. 'I'm happy to see you here today, ah... Khan! Where are the others?'

'My brother is here, Sir, but my mother and sister did not come,' he replied, slightly embarrassed.

'That's a pity,' said the Reverend. 'Did you enjoy our service? I trust that next week we will have a bigger crowd. About your request, my boy, I'm afraid I won't be of much help to you in your new enterprise. But, I can purchase whatever foodstuff my wife needs from you. Most of my friends employ workers to grow their own foodstuff; however, if you need transportation to the market, I can send Carl with the wagon to meet you on Saturday morning.'

'Thank you, Sir,' replied Sanwar. 'My brother and I made a box cart, but thank you so much, Sir, for your offer.'

When Sanwar left the schoolyard that Sunday, he was too disappointed to join in conversation with his brother and sister. In spite of what the Reverend had told him, he would still pursue his plans. He hoped that even if business was slow at the start, eventually it would be profitable. His family was dependent on him and success was his goal. He would not be discouraged and would still make preparations to sell his family produce at the market. Manwar and a group of children had walked on and left him behind. He couldn't avoid feeling so helpless; his entire family were all so helpless without his father. His dear mother suffered the most, he thought. Often, she would sit silently among them as if far away, rapt in the memory of his father. Sanwar knew he had to do his best, at least for her.

On Saturday morning, Carl arrived promptly at six o'clock. The boys had already collected their produce and left them overnight in the box cart. Eagerly, Carl helped to transfer the vegetables to the wagon – pumpkins, cabbage, spinach, string beans, melongenes, ochroes, coconuts, fresh seasoning and hot peppers. When Carl quickly picked up the latter, Manwar shouted, 'Careful wid dat, yuh go get blind if dat pepper jus' touch yuh eye, Carl!'

Carl smiled. Manwar was so excited, that every other item he took up fell out of his hands. Sanwar was quiet and apprehensive. He spoke softly to Carl, 'what you t'ink Carl, you t'ink we will sell all this?' He gestured in the direction of the laden wagon.

'Well,' said Carl, his hands resting comfortably on his hips. 'I t'ink so – but we have to go now. All de people does come to market early. By de time de sun get hot everybody done gone home. All de white missus and dem don't like de sun to burn dere skin.'

Carl peered through his fingers at the rising sun, its position summoning the boys to leave. They boarded the wagon and the mule paced forward. Indrani watched them move forward slowly until Carl struck the animal, causing it to increase its pace into a trot. 'Hi, hi!' he shouted. The trot developed quickly into a brisk, steady run. Sanwar and his brother were jerked into the awareness that they were finally on their way to the market. Indrani clapped, wishing them a productive day, while Gariban stared helplessly as the wagon disappeared. Her daughter, observing Gariban's demeanour offered words of comfort, 'Don't worry, Mai; everything go be aw' right. Bhai and Beta is good boys. Come on inside now and leh we make lunch for dem; dey go be hungry when dey come back.'

Gariban climbed the steps slowly, her tear-filled eyes partly blinding her vision as she entered the room. She did not lack confidence in her sons, but the emotional torture of observing their struggle with life at such a tender age haunted her.

At the market, the boys were surprised to see so many vendors. Most of them were East Indians like themselves, who sold their foodstuff on Saturdays before going to the plantations to work. They were assisted by their children, mainly boys, who helped arrange the produce on sheets of old newsprint and pieces of discarded sugar bags. Vendors displayed their vegetables along the roadside. Manwar did not think of taking a *pera*, a low stool, for Sanwar and himself to sit on and so they were forced to stand or stoop while waiting for customers.

Most customers bought only a few items. Sanwar discovered that green vegetables were in greater demand than ground provisions, which were grown by every free African. At the market, there was also Maharaj, the owner of a rice mill who sold cups of rice, which he dipped out of the heavy rice bag. This commodity was the staple food of the East Indians. The shoppers comprised mainly women. The white women selected the commodities they wanted and paid for them, while their African female helpers carried the boxes and baskets containing their purchased items. Although household owners employed workers to grow ground provisions, fresh green and leafy vegetables could be bought only at the market. These items complemented the local Sunday meal to the advantage of Sanwar and his brother. Sanwar was not much of a businessman, but his brother grasped the chance to prove himself a talented farmer. He stopped the customers to ask them to buy a wedge of pumpkin and proudly commented on the bright yellow colour, a manifestation of excellent quality. He offered to take the heavy items to their waiting wagons. While Sanwar carried on with the sales, Manwar became so enthused that he decided to take charge of collecting and counting the coins – the precious few, which he looked forward to taking home to his mother.

By ten o'clock, the buyers had almost completely disappeared and the two boys decided to go home. All the foodstuff had been sold, except for the hot peppers which remained scorching in the sun.

'How much money we make, Bhai?' asked the younger boy.

'Four shillings and two pennies – that is one dollar,' answered his big brother.

'Yuh t'ink dat good? Yuh t'ink Mai go be happy wid dat?' he asked excitedly.

'I hope so,' replied Sanwar. 'Dat is de best we could do.'

They trudged along wearily but contentedly, Manwar pushing the box cart along with the peppers and Sanwar holding the sales of their produce close to his chest. The walk was long and tiring, but they chatted about their first experience at the market until they arrived home.

Indrani was sitting on the steps awaiting her brothers' return. The scraping of the box-cart wheels caught her attention; then, she glimpsed Sanwar's head bobbing up and down as he climbed the brow of the hill.

'Mai, Mai!' she shouted. 'Dey coming now, dey coming!' She ran as if with the speed of flight and grabbed on to them both, one arm almost encircling each boy's waist. Wide-eyed and curious, she peered into the box-cart inquiringly.

'Everything sell Bhai, Manwar?' She stared each boy in the face, clapped her hands exultantly, and holding on to them securely for support, jumped into the air repeatedly. She accompanied them to the house, looking very pleased with herself, as if she too, was part of their achievement.

Gariban was overjoyed at her sons' success. As an expression of her appreciation, she led them quickly to the small table, fussing over them as she served the midday meal. Indrani shared her mother's enthusiasm helping to make her brothers as comfortable as possible. All eyes centred on the heroes of the day. Gariban was so overwhelmed, she kept heaping rice onto Manwar's already full plate.

'Dat enough, Mai, I cyah eat more dan dat!' he exclaimed. 'Keep some for later.'

It was the first time since Ackbar's death that the family had shared such a measure of contentment.

Sanwar resumed classes at school every morning,

but promptly returned home at lunchtime to help his brother with the garden. The number of students in his class had increased considerably during his absence. There were now twenty students and Mr Gill was kept fully occupied. Reverend Thompson was obliged to take a more active part in teaching the students how to read and write, but he did not neglect religious education. He continuously walked around with his Bible and made the children repeat after him, line by line, the Bible passages he read them. Sometimes the extracts made sense, and sometimes they were unintelligible to the children. But, the Reverend made sure that the stories about Jesus were kept interesting and lively in their memories.

One morning, a ten-year-old Muslim boy informed the Reverend that Jesus was only a prophet, but that Mohammet was God's final messenger. He was the bravest of all God's messengers and had united his people before his death. The boy's father had told him that the only great God was Allah and that there was only one God. Khalim, the young boy, was not insolent; he was only repeating what he had been taught. Reverend Thompson was surprised at Khalim's knowledge and frankness, and refrained from pursuing the topic further. It was obvious that the boy's father was a devout Muslim and that he objected to his son being influenced by an alien religion. With the exception of Khalim, Sanwar was the only other Muslim present. Reverend Thompson made no comment. The next day, Khalim's absence from class was conspicuous.

Sanwar continued to devote as much time as he

could to reading, writing and solving the arithmetical problems upon which Mr Gill gave the class to work. He made remarkable improvement in these subjects and Mr Gill often requested that he read aloud for the younger children. Sometimes, it was necessary to divide them in two or three groups because of their numbers and age differences. Sanwar had developed a habit of staying on for an hour or so longer than he had before, to help the younger students. Occasionally, they asked him to tell them a story about Jesus, which they remembered from, *Life of Jesus* – a collection of stories written by a Canadian Minister. The stories were interesting and he became more engrossed in the exercise of reading proficiently than in the religious implications of the contents.

Now at fourteen, Sanwar thought very seriously about his future. A vast gulf existed between the world from which he came and the world in which he presently lived. He wished he could have followed the beliefs of his parents, but the new religion was offering him an opportunity he could not refuse. He was entering a world which seemed to promise rewards. He was yet unsure about his future, but he was willing to seize any prospect to improve his situation and help his family recover from their recent tragedy. He was now the senior male in his family and he had to make a responsible decision. One mind beckoned him to the future; the other recalled him to the past. He dared not reveal his innermost deliberations to his mother. In spite of his dilemma, he was fully conscious of one burning desire – to alter his lowly status as the son of an indentured immigrant.

Rose-grey skies heralded the break of dawn. The earthy smell of early morning showers roused the brothers from slumber. Drowsily, Sanwar rose and removed the bent rod which held open the hinged wooden shutter. In a few minutes, both boys rolled up their thin fibre mattresses, tied them into cylindrical shapes and leaned them in a corner of the room. No time could be wasted on market day. Khalim would soon come to meet them. He too was a market vendor and sold some commodities from his father's shop.

Later that day, Sanwar counted the day's earnings: six shillings, four pennies and two farthings. One huge uncut pumpkin only remained. Mai could always use this, he thought; but fortunately, all the green vegetables were sold – ochroes, *bodi*, *bhagi*, lettuce, heaps of seasonings and callaloo bush – which the cooks from the great houses bought. The boys needed to purchase some split peas and flour to take home. Manwar was about to pay Khalim for the two commodities, when Khalim, in a high-spirited mood blurted out, 'I dohn want no money for dat, boy. Tell yuh Mai I give she dat present today. Jus' go and pack up yuh t'ings. All yuh sell everyt'ing, Manwar? Yuh should open a shop now!'

Khalim seemed to be in great haste to leave the market scene. He was packing utensils and half-filled bags of peas, rice and flour clumsily onto the donkey cart. His gait and general demeanour revealed he was seething with excitement.

'All yuh Khan boys slow today eh? Bhai, yuh dreamin' or what? Ah have plenty wuk to do home. Mai say to reach home by t'ree o'clock,' he continued.

'Eh-heh, so w'at is de big secret, Khalim – like yuh getting married today or w'at?' asked Manwar. The boys exploded in laughter.

'Yuh mad boy!' screamed Khalim. 'Mai cooking food from dis morning. Meh Baap whole family come from Princes Town – tonight dey breaking de fast and tomorrow is *Eid*. Dey bring a *imam* too. I forget to tell yuh. Mai say to tell yuh Mai and Indrani to come by we tonight. Yuh want to come too, Bhai, Manwar?'

Khalim did not wait for an answer. He proceeded to untie the donkey while Manwar and his brother climbed onto the cart. Khalim raced the animal all the way until he approached the Maracas hill, then along the pathway which led to the Khans' household. Manwar was the first to enter the hut and found his mother in the kitchen. On hearing the good news, Gariban was overjoyed.

'Tomorrow is *Eid*! Chile what yuh saying? Is like a dream come true, a real *imam*! Is like going back home and praying wid de whole family togedder! If only yuh Baap was here wid us. Allah keep him safe, be good to meh husband.'

Tears came to her eyes as she drifted into the past. Manwar broke the silence, 'Mai, yuh want me to help do anyt'ing?'

Sanwar handed over the coins which he had folded in a piece of old newspaper. She stared at them intently, slowly regaining her presence of mind.

'Indrani, where yuh?' She slowly turned around to face her daughter. 'Come, we have to make some *dhalpouri* and *mithai* to carry tonight – we cyah go empty hand. Manwar, light de fire quick. Indrani put de peas to boil. Indrani! Make haste! Tonight go be a bless night. If only yuh Baap was here. We must pray for him.'

Gariban uttered, in ecstasy, breathless praise and gratitude to Allah, the Hoseins, her newly found friends, her dearly departed Ackbar and her children. Manwar smiled as he watched his elated mother move in circles, fidgeting with familiar kitchen utensils. Slowly and silently, Sanwar walked to the front of the hut and sat on the wooden steps. When Gariban and Indrani were ready to leave for the Hoseins', the boys accompanied them to the house and returned home. It had been a long time since they had the opportunity to be together in private.

The two brothers sat for a while and stared at the clear, blue haze radiated by the crescent moon and star, a holy night for all Muslims. On a night like this, Ackbar was buried alongside two fellow workmen when the giant immortelle crashed onto the cocoa and coffee plantation. Their silence was uncomfortable. To Manwar his brother seemed distant, as though he was troubled by his own thoughts – nothing physical, yet it affected his appearance and interaction with family members. Bhai was now the head of the household; he had to protect them all. Of course he, Manwar, would help and work as hard as ever – but Bhai was the leader. Maybe this was Sanwar's problem. Manwar intended to find out tonight.

'Yuh find it hot tonight, Bhai?' Manwar asked his brother, trying to break the silence.

'No, not hot, jus' a little still, no breeze. We have to collect more water for de plants, or else dey go dry up,' replied Sanwar.

'Is a good night doh for Khalim family. Dey build a tent outside to cook, and for de children to play after de prayers. Ah so glad for Mai; I wish it had a Mosque close by and a *imam*. I know she miss hearing Baap reading for she. Bhai, yuh okay? Somet'ing troubling yuh? Ah know yuh have work to do in de school and Mr Gill want yuh to be a Christian, but Bhai, yuh dohn have to be a Christian like dem. Khalim learn to read and write but he still a Muslim.' Manwar was trying to be supportive.

'Dey want to give me a work to teach children to read and write – down South – but I dohn know how to tell Mai,' replied Sanwar.

'Reverend Thompson cyah do dat to yuh Bhai; yuh cyah leave yuh family like dat and go. How yuh going to eat? Who go wash for yuh and cook for yuh? Yuh is jus' a young boy; yuh cyah go dong South wit'out us!'

Manwar was upset. He could not bear the thought of having his only brother, his big brother, leave home.

'The Reverend in San Fernando, Reverend Hall, tell Reverend Thompson I could get a teaching work at a new school, just outside San Fernando. I want to go, Manwar, but I want all of us to go... you, Mai and Indrani. I not going to leave you. I want all of us to go at de same time, but when? I dohn really know. I just cyah face Mai. I can see more problems in dis dan just de work, Manwar. You know how Mai feel about de new religion and me getting mix up wit' Christians. I feel so bad about de whole situation. But if both of we could get work down South, dat would be de best t'ing dat ever happen to us. I beginning to t'ink dat up here dohn have a future for us, Beta. Mai look so sad, so lonely.'

'If only,' interrupted Manwar. 'Mai had friends and places to go. She cyah even go to Port of Spain to see de stores. An we self, we cyah even talk English good. From de time yuh start to show yuh pass de people shouting, 'Wey dem coolie going! Bhai, yuh know somet'ing? Ah agree wit' yuh,' said Manwar, as tears filled his eyes. 'We go make we own future but mos' of all, we mus' stay together.'

Gariban and Indrani stayed overnight at the Hoseins' and returned home just before nine o'clock the following morning. The boys were still asleep. Gariban carefully arranged a small breakfast of *sawine*, an Indian delicacy, and sweetmeats which Khalim's mother had given her. She made some tea and sent Indrani to awaken the boys when the small table was laid. Although exhausted from staying up all night, she was so happy. As the brothers approached, she greeted them in true Muslim fashion, *Assalam u Alaikum Eid Mubarak*. They returned the greeting and hugged each other. Gariban took time off from her kitchen chores to relate the night's events and share her recently acquired knowledge of Princes Town. She was so excited about having met Imam Ali and Khalim's uncle who had made her an offer. To her, Kamal Hosein seemed to be wealthy as he was the eldest brother of the Hosein family.

'What offer?' asked Sanwar.

'He say if we want to buy a piece o' land he could sell, or if meh sons want to work for him – he have a rice field and a mill and he could rent we a small place until we get we own house.'

'What about a work in de sugar plantation – in Usine Mai?' asked Manwar. 'Ah could get a work dere?'

'Yuh could cut cane?' retorted his mother. 'Yuh have eleven years – yuh could help in de cane field but yuh cyah cut cane. Maybe yuh could help Khalim uncle in de rice mill: and Bhai, what yuh go do – yuh go come wid us, or yuh staying here wid de new church?' Gariban asked her elder son. Sanwar was dumbfounded. His mother had caught him by surprise. She was aware of much more than he realised. He knew he had to give her an answer.

'No Mai, I not staying in Maracas. I going down South wit' you,' he muttered.

Gariban was relieved, at least for the time being. Khalim's uncle would be staying in St Joseph for the next two weeks. The *imam* wanted to build a Mosque in the north. At least she had some time to think about moving.

The rainy season forewarned the Khan boys that their crops were in danger. The grey, threatening clouds came early. May thunderstorms replaced May flowers. Manwar and Bhai worked in the garden continuously. The corn was too young to be reaped and there would not be enough time for it to mature before these early rains came. Heaps of ochroes, *bodi*, pigeon peas – some already worm-eaten, tomatoes and corn took up residence in the small wooden building. Only the sleeping area was spared. Indrani helped stack the bags and containers that the boys brought inside.

Gariban reminded her sons to cut enough carat leaves to mend the roof. Old pieces of flat worn metal, galvanise and tarpaulin were used to aid the run-off from heavy downpours. Dry wood was another priority. The ladies wandered around nearby bushes for dried sticks and fallen branches. They piled these in heaps while the boys cut them into manageable sizes and then packed them in a corner of the makeshift porch.

Maracas looked foreboding. The clouds were thick and grey and then the rains came. The river flooded its banks, spreading red muddy clay into the villagers' yards. A reddish-brown hue covered the entire land-scape. Small animals and poultry were enclosed in temporary pens made of sticks and branches while cows, donkeys and horses were tied to tree trunks. For one week, villagers who attempted to cross the swirling river were forced to retreat to their homes without success. Maracas village was practically isolated.

When the rain stopped and the water subsided, Sanwar and his brother took their foodstuff to market for sale. When there was a lull in customers, Sanwar left his brother for a short while to wander around and inquire about the school. He wondered if the books and furniture were washed away. He missed the children's chatter and bustle. He missed reading for them, missed their close attention and their steady gaze. They often clapped when he had concluded reading a story for them from the Reverend's collection of stories about Jesus. His new role as an assistant teacher gave him a thrill of achievement. If only it was possible for him to pursue that dream of becoming an educated man. He was jolted out of his reverie by Khalim.

'Ah Bhai, ah going to Tunapuna for Baap. Yuh want to come?' he invited. 'I hear de school flood and everyt'ing float away. Tell Manwar to wait 'till we come back.'

Sanwar explained his family's plight to Khalim; he and his brother were hoping to sell the produce they had brought to market. Everything else was destroyed in the flood.

'All ah we in de same boat, Bhai. Ah going now to collect some vegetables from Baap garden in Tunapuna – odderwise we starve next week. Baap say if he didn't have de shop he would pack up and go to live in Princes Town. Mai say she hear de Tunapuna Orphanage in shambles; de children had to sleep in de church. Come, make haste – Rahim waiting for me already.'

Sanwar's heart sank when he saw the state of the classrooms. Furniture and books were stuck in the mud, which had piled up high against the walls. The most obvious colour was red – from clay which covered the floors and the entire yard. It was like a sea of red clay. He stood speechless as though hypnotised. He was numb; his mind was blank. He wondered what could happen next.

After the flood, Gariban decided to leave Maracas. She asked Khalim's father to advertise the sale of her property in his shop. She was positive she would get an early response since many indentured immigrants were becoming peasant farmers and worked on the plantations only part-time. Sanwar wrote the advertisement on a piece of cardboard in large, capital charcoal letters and nailed it onto Mr Hosein's shop door.

Within one week, three prospective buyers had expressed interest in purchasing Gariban's property. Khalim and Manwar were instrumental in this development. They advertised the property verbally to residents, whom they thought might be interested in purchasing it. This strategy was necessary also because most indentured immigrants were illiterate – the advertisement on Mr Hosein's shop door was meaningless to them.

Rahim was a prospective buyer of Gariban's property. He worked for Khalim's father, selling vegetables at the Tunapuna market. He often served as a handyman around the shop. In the second half of the year, during the planting and growing periods of sugar cane, he was employed on the Mausica plantation. Rahim had lost both his parents soon after his arrival in Trinidad and had grown up in the Tunapuna orphanage from the age of six. Now at the age of twenty, he was tired of being single and thought of settling down to family life.

Another potential buyer, Soogrim, Ackbar's contemporary, still worked on Mr Dickinson's cocoa and coffee plantation in the Maracas hills. He lived in the barracks with a fourteen-year-old son and a five-year-old daughter. His wife, Halgee, had died in childbirth five years ago. Soogrim had served two terms of indentureship in Trinidad.

Babu was the third interested buyer. He was about sixty years old and lived with his wife, Meena, in

Tacarigua. It was rumoured that Babu was wealthy, although his physical carriage did not support this rumour. His frequent visits to the forest prompted the villagers to believe that he hid his fortune in a secret forest tree. His interest in purchasing her property puzzled Gariban; nevertheless, she was not prepared to tolerate any delay in her relocation to Princes Town.

She decided to sell to Soogrim, whom she knew best of all three men. He was responsible, industrious and more importantly, she was positive he could afford to pay her cash immediately. Two weeks after her property was advertised, it was sold and Gariban was ready to move to South Trinidad.

CHAPTER 2

Moving On

A new dawn breaks on high
I see a radiance
An unknown faith
A strange world unfolds
To discover and explore.
This Challenge I embrace,
This web of experience,
A future ahead.
Grant me, dear Father
Courage, strength and wisdom
To build my destiny
A search for knowledge,
Steadfast faith
And home, at last.

When Mai get a sale for de property, Bhai and me decide to clean up de yard, burn de dry leaves and rotten wood, and stack up all de firewood in de shed. Bhai say Soogrim would be glad for dat – he could do wit' de help as he was getting down in strength. Indrani and Mai was so busy cooking, cleaning and packing during the day dat Bhai and me had talk to dem only during mealtime. Mai pack up de pots and pans, and enamel bowls and cups in a cardboard box, and put all de clothes in a bundle. Indrani wanted to take de two goats to Princes Town, but Mai say she not travelling on de train with any animal in case de conductor put we off de train. Indrani make a fuss and start to cry, so Mai decide to leave de goats with Khalim's fadder and say if Indrani want to come back to Tunapuna for de goats she could do dat. Khalim mudder, Ma Hosein, promise to keep a kid for Indrani because de female was having young ones.

De day before we leave Maracas, Bhai hug all o' we and say he would come to Princes Town as soon as he settle his business, meaning getting work and a place to live. Carl take Bhai to de train station in his cart and I went to see him off. Bhai wrap de garden tools in a big sugar bag and tie it wit' a piece o' rope. He say he would bring dem for us de day after we reach Princes Town.

De next day Mai, me, Indrani, Khalim's Auntie Deedee and Khalim's cousin Nat' travel by train to San Fernando, den by cart to Princes Town. Mohan was de driver and he used to work for Khalim's uncle, Sayeed.

De Hosein family was big and dey was wealt'y. Besides Nat' and his parents, two odder uncles and aunts, dere children and grandparents all used to live in de same house. Dey used to live upstairs, and downstairs Khalim's uncle had a shop, just like Khalim's fadder in Tunapuna. One of Khalim's uncles was a *imam*, and one was in charge of a rice mill and all de workers on a farm close by. De Hosein family had cows and goats, and sheep and horses, and carts and buggies.

Mai and me and Indrani stay wit' de Hoseins for two weeks. It look like Mai make a kind o' bargain wit' Khalim's uncle for me to work on dere farm. Indrani and Mai help in de kitchen and Khalim's Auntie Deedee make time to show de ladies 'round Princes Town. Mai say she would buy a piece o' land for we to build a small house and still have enough land to grow vegetables. In de meantime, I could work for de Hoseins and when I get a little bigger, I could work for de sugar factory part-time.

Bhai and Boodoo come to see us de day after we went to Princes Town. Boodoo was Reverend Hall's buggy driver and he was waiting on de Reverend who was visiting de school in Princes Town. He and Bhai had a few hours to spare and decide to spend some time wit' us.

'Why yuh dohn stay here in Princes Town, Bhai, and teach in de school here?' I ask him.

'The school here has enough teachers, Beta; but the Church is opening more schools in San Fernando. The Reverend said he wants me to go to the Teachers' College and that is in San Fernando,' Bhai explain. 'Besides, you want Mai to die or what – with two different religions in the same house!'

'Sorry Bhai, I jus' not t'inking! Is jus' dat I go miss having you 'round de place. Yuh have only fourteen years and yuh teaching children to read and write!' I say to him.

'Yeh,' replied Sanwar. 'And I am learning too; I have a long way to go. Only now, I am starting to teach in a real school. The Canaan school is a small one, you know. Most of the time, the children don't want to come to school and we have to go and get them from their barracks or the cane field,' he tell me.

'So why dey forcing de poor children to read and write; why dey dohn leave dem alone?' I ask.

'This place belongs to the English, Beta; this is not India. Here the children have to learn English and write like the English man, otherwise they're not getting anywhere – education, they call it, Beta.'

Mai and Indrani was too busy with de morning housework, so Bhai say a quick *Salaam* to de family. Khalim's Uncle Sayeed wrap up a few t'ings in a paper for Bhai and tell him to take care of hisself and dat he could come to see Mai and Indrani and me anytime. Khalim's Auntie Deedee give Bhai some *roti* and *baigan* to carry wid him. Poor Bhai, he had to cook for his own self now. Tears swell up in Mai eyes when Bhai was leaving, but she just went in de kitchen to hide she face. Me and Indrani decide to visit Bhai de next Saturday afternoon when he didn't have school.

Bhai was teaching in a small Christian school just outside San Fernando, not far from de Crossroads where dere was a big junction. At dis place, the train line from Princes Town was crossing de road leaving San Fernando and going to Bhai's school in Canaan. Dat same road, Bhai say, went further down sout' to Debe and Penal and Point Fortin. Even on Saturday, children went to school – for Bible class. To me, Bhai work every day; but on Saturday afternoon, he had time to wash his clothes, read, and get to know San Fernando better. De area where he was living was famous for troublemaking cane cutters. Years before we had move to Princes Town, de Muslims celebrating

Hosay went against de town order and march to San Fernando with huge *tadjahs*. Dey insist on carrying dese huge decorations even doh dey know dey was breaking de law. The police fire guns and kill some people, and injure hundreds of Muslims. Mai warn me and Indrani not to 'walk all about' and to stay wit' Bhai until it was time to meet Mohan by de train station. Bhai introduce me and Indrani to two friends, Gopee and Jai. Dey was teachers too and did convert to de new religion – so I feel Bhai would join de church soon. Bhai was lucky dat Jai like to cook, so he and Gopee make a garden behind de barracks where dey was living and keep de place tidy. Around four o'clock dat evening, we walk to de train station near de wharf in San Fernando to meet Mohan to go back to Princes Town. Of de five of us, Bhai was de shortest; even Indrani was taller dan Bhai. All de same, I was sure he was de smartest in all of us. Mohan was driving a mule cart. He had just drop off four passengers at de station and was talking to a young Negro boy standing on de pavement. De boy was asking Mohan for a ride back to Princes Town because he had miss de las' train. Bhai and his two friends leave us to go home and me and Indrani step up in de cart.

'What yuh doing down here by yuhself, Will?' ask Mohan.

'I come to bring some ground provisions for Pappy and de train lef' me. Ah lucky to see you doh!' say Will, his broad smile showing off a mouth full of big teeth.

'Come up, man; dis is Manwar and he sister, Indrani. Dey living Princes Town now; dey used to live up Nort' before,' say Mohan.

'And my name is Will – William Fowell Thompson. Hope yuh like Princes Town,' say Will. He seem to be a pleasant boy.

'Where yuh get a name like dat?' I ask him. He didn't look very English to me.

'Oh! meh grandpappy give me dat name after a cotton planter he know in America,' answer Will.

'So yuh is ah American?' I ask him. I was confuse.

'Not me, but my grandpappy and my pappy and my maw born in America, and come to Trinidad a long time ago after all de slaves get free,' he say.

'Boy, Princes Town is like a little world in itself; it have all kind o' people,' I tell him. 'What kind o' work yuh does do Will?' I ask him.

'Oh I help Pappy with everyt'ing – pick cocoa, drive de cart, make garden and I go to school too,' he say.

'Go to school, which school?' I ask again.

'De Anglican School – but my religion is Baptist from way back in Grandpappy days,' he continue.

'Yuh grandpappy still alive, Will?' I ask him again. I had just realise dat of all de young boys I know only Bhai and me didn't have a Baap or Dada.

'My grandpappy is ninety-two years old and is still full o' words,' he say, smiling.

'What a lucky boy you is, Will!' I say to him. 'Yuh dohn know how lucky yuh is.'

When Indrani and me reach Khalim's uncle house, Mai was in deep conversation with Khalim's Uncle Sayeed and Auntie Deedee. I sense dat Mai wanted to buy a piece o' land and build a carat house, and find some work, whatever she could do. So Khalim's Uncle Sayeed and Mai went to see a rich Hindu man, name

Bopal. Mohan say Bopal was getting old now and had plenty land with sugar cane growing; but since de price of sugar went down, it was hard to get people to grow cane for him. So, he might sell Mai a plot o' land. Mohan say Bopal didn't have children and dat was a big problem. His wife was old and sickly, and he had a feeling Bopal wanted a new wife – but dat was anodder problem. So Mai and Khalim's Uncle Sayeed went to see Bopal early one Sunday morning, when dey was sure Bopal was still home because he used to wake up early every morning except on Sunday and go to de cane field. Mai was lucky to meet him and Bopal start to relate his problems as soon as dey begin to talk to him.

'Dem people dohn want to work for me,' complain Bopal. 'Dey want dey own land now. It dohn make sense growing so much cane. Dese days I minding animals – horses, buffalo, mules to draw de cart and carry cane to de factory, and cocoa to de cocoa centre. We carrying people too, in de buggies, plenty movement from Princes Town to San Fernando. De Usine factory still making sugar. Now cocoa have money and ah wish ah had de strength to grow cocoa, but as yuh see, ah getting old now.'

Mai say after Bopal tell dem his whole life story, he agree to sell she two acres o' land for fifty dollars. It was sugar cane land, but it was crop time and de workers did cut de cane already. Khalim's uncle carry Mai to de Warden's office to sign a paper to make sure dat Mai was de new owner, and den we start cleaning up de land to build we own little carat house in Princes Town.

One afternoon about five o'clock, a donkey cart stop in front de carat house. I was sitting on a *pera* outside, stripping a coconut branch to make a cocoyea broom for Mai and I was so surprise to see it was Mr Bopal stepping down from de cart. He was using a walking stick to balance his steps. It seem dat it was a long day for him – he look tired and worried. He walk towards me and ask me to call Mai. She did hear him come and when I was about to get up to call Mai, I see dat she was already standing in de doorway.

He walk up to she and say, 'Madam Khan, I come to tell yuh I have a job for yuh two children. De cane field and dem want a cleaning and manuring – to plant for next season so maybe yuh son would like to do dat work. Ah know he young and cyah cut cane yet, but he go get used to working on de land and later on he could do a big man work,' Bopal say.

'How much yuh paying him Mr Bopal?' Mai ask.

'W-e-ll, t'-r-e-e shil-lings a week,' he say stretching out his words.

'He have to work de whole day from Monday to Saturday?' Mai question him, not believing she ears.

'Yes, until all de fields clean and manure,' Bopal say.

'I t'ink yuh could give meh son at least five shillings for de week, Mister Bopal; de factory paying a shilling a day to manure cane. Manwar could start from tomorrow if yuh want!' Mai went on, 'Yuh say yuh have work for meh two children, but I dohn really want Indrani to work in de cane field. Is true she older dan Beta, but I would like she to get work in de house.'

'Well, Madam Khan – she can work in meh house,' he say. 'Meh wife does suffer wit' bad art'ritis. She does get bad pain in she joints and she does have too much trouble to knead de flour and wash de clothes and clean up de kitchen. So what if yuh daughter help with de kitchen work and around de place?' he ask Mai. Mai give a little dry smile.

Mai call Indrani and me from de back o' de house. We was listening to every word and Indrani was pretending she was washing de dirty enamel plates we use for dinner before Mr Bopal arrive. Indrani was confuse and speechless, but I was excited.

When we come out in front o' de house, Bopal examine Indrani from head to toe, den ask, 'How old she is, Mai?'

'Sixteen years, Mister Bopal – she never work before. She is meh only girl child, so treat she good.'

When de first week finish, Indrani come home wit' two shillings, some *roti* and a bag full o' *baigan*. Mai didn't have to worry about cooking food for Indrani because it look like Bopal had plenty food, but somehow Indrani didn't look too happy. Mai tell she to be grateful to Allah for his mercies – she not starving and getting wet, and she still have family to worry about she.

'But Mai, Ma Bopal have more dan art'ritis,' she say to Mai.

'What yuh mean by dat?' Mai ask she.

'De two o' dem have a nasty cough. In de morning, and in de evening before I leave to come home, Ma Bopal cyah stop coughing and spitting, and beating she chest like she have heart trouble,' she say, looking very upset.

'And what about Bopal, Beti?' Mai ask. She was starting to get worried.

'Two t'ings trouble me about dat man, Mai; one is dat he coughing bad too, and Mai, I could feel him staring at me from de corner of he eye when meh back turn. I try not to have any talk wid him but he is de one paying me,' she say, trying to explain de situation.

'Dohn pay him no mind and stay far from him,' Mai advise. 'Keep close to Ma Bopal until is time to leave de house and come home.'

One Saturday evening, me and Indrani went to Khalim's Uncle Sayeed's shop to buy *dhal* and flour for Mai. Den, we meet Bhai. He was going to see de Reverend in de church and get a ride wit' him to San Fernando. Bhai didn't look happy. He say dat he went to see Mai and dat she was so upset when he tell she he was going to get baptise. She start to cry and pray to Allah to forgive him, and she couldn't stop talking about Baap turning in de grave, if he know dat his big son changing to de Christian religion. Anyway, Bhai tell Indrani and me to come to de Presbyterian Church on Coffee Street to de baptism service de next Sunday. After dat, de Reverend wife was making lunch for de converts and dere close family.

'And you are the only family I have Beta – you and Indrani,' Bhai say. 'You know Mai will never come. You don't have to feel guilty because only Indians will be in the church. Gopee and Jai will be there. I will tell them to look out for you and Indrani. Now, don't forget – I am expecting both of you.'

When we reach home, me and Indrani pass 'round de back of de house to be on de safe side. We could hear Mai talking loud, half singing and half crying, and beating she chest and sighing. After waiting outside for a few minutes, Indrani say, 'Beta, we may as well go inside; it getting dark and Mai go be worrying about we.'

Mai was only too glad to let out all she feelings when we reach de house. 'You t'ink dat is right, Beta? Bhai go and join de Christian Church! I dohn mind if he learn Hindi and English, and teach in de school, but to leave de religion he born in – dat he mudder and fadder believe in, and turn he back on we! Allah forgive yuh, meh son. Yuh fadder mus' be crying in de grave. So dis is what dis new land, dis Trinidad do to meh family. It divide we; it bring pain! It take meh husband away and give meh big son to de white man, de same white man we fight against in India and run away from. Ah, Bhai! He gone away too – for ever.'

De next day, Sunday, Indrani and me wake up early to go to Bhai's baptism. Indrani say to Mai dat she want to go because Bhai only have two people in de whole of Trinidad to depend on. Dat make Mai quiet for a while. She just shake she head, as if she was trying to understand Bhai's side of de story – but just couldn't.

Me and Indrani was a little early at de church. De people who had to get baptise was dere already, including Bhai. De Reverend was explaining somet'ing to dem. Just den, Gopee and Jai see we and bring we to sit inside at de front o' de church. On de left side, some white women and children was sitting on benches. On de right side, dere was some empty benches where Jai say de new converts would sit. Me, Indrani, Gopee and Jai was sitting behind de empty seats. We could hear de people towards de back talking in Hindustani.

'De white Reverend talking in Hindi today, Jai?' I ask.

'Not today, Beta,' he answer.

'So how all dese people go understand him?' I say.

'Dohn worry,' he say. 'They will understand; the Indian Reverend going to give the sermon today in Hindi, but the white one going to baptise the converts.'

A white lady start to play church music and everybody stand up. Bhai give us a quick wave and smile. He look happy dat me and Indrani come after all. Den, de white Reverend say a prayer and lead de singing from a book he was holding open. He announce it was time to start baptizing de new converts. Bhai had dress up nice and clean in a white shirt, black tie, black pants and black shoes. We see twelve converts in all. Bhai was second in line. Each convert had to kneel and de Reverend pour some water on dere head and say dere names.

After de first one get baptise, Bhai step foward and kneel in front o' de Reverend. Den, de Reverend place one hand on Bhai's forehead and say, loud enough for everybody to hear, 'Clarence Stephen Sanowar McKenzie, I baptise thee in the name of the Father and the Son and the Holy Spirit and sign thee with the sign of the cross.' Den, he pour some water on Bhai's head. Me and Indrani stare into one anodder face.

'Wait till Mai hear dis,' say Indrani.

'Dohn say a word to Mai, yuh hear me?' I warn she. But, de change in Bhai's name trouble me from dat time. I never hear one odder word in de church after dat. I only see a Indian man dress up in coat and tie, walk to one side o' de church, open a big book, put it on a small, high table and read about Jesus. He talk for a long time. Den, we stand up, listen to people singing and praying, and sit dong again. When de church service was over, de first t'ing I do was to ask Bhai, 'But Bhai, you and me is still brudders. How come you have a different name from me now? You have to change yuh name too?'

'Don't worry about that, Beta. We will always be brothers,' he say. Den, he hug meh shoulders and look in meh face. 'Come, is time for us to eat somet'ing; I am sure you and Indrani are hungry,' he tell we.

'And, Bhai?' I ask him again. 'Where de Reverend get all dese names to give yuh?'

Bhai smile and say dat was a long story. 'Well, Beta, you see, I think Mai and Baap travelled from India on the boat named Clarence, and so I chose that name. The Reverend chose the name Stephen, who is one of the first Christians in the Bible, and McKenzie is the name of the Reverend who is teaching me in the Bible Study class,' Bhai answer.

'Bhai,' I say again, 'maybe when dey give yuh all dese names yuh bound to stay in de Christian church. Maybe yuh can never be a Muslim again.' Bhai didn't say nothing else. He jus' smile and we went to de Church Hall to eat lunch.

Indrani continue to work for Mr Bopal. She stop complaining as much as before, but it look like she was afraid o' somet'ing. One evening when she reach home, she tell me and Mai dat Ma Bopal fall sick and Mr Bopal call a old Indian woman to make medicine for she and rub she down.

'What happen to Ma Bopal, chile, she have a cold?' Mai ask.

'No, Mai, she was coughing and spitting blood,' say Indrani.

Mai face change and say it sound serious, so she

decide to go to help Mr Bopal de next day. Besides, she didn't want Indrani to be dere alone wit'out a big woman in de house. Mr Bopal wait t'ree days to see if Ma Bopal would get better and when he realise Ma Bopal was only getting worse, he get scared and went to Princes Town to find a doctor. It was after lunchtime when Mr Bopal and de doctor step down from de cart. De doctor was a light brown-skinned man wit' curly hair. Mai say he was polite and say 'good afternoon' when he walk in de house. By de time de doctor get there, Ma Bopal had stop talking. He examine Ma Bopal for a few minutes, den ask Mai to wash his hands.

'Spitting blood – severe coughing – very high temperature… This is tuberculosis,' he say. 'How long has she been like this?' de Doctor ask Mr Bopal.

'A week, Sah,' he answer.

'Give her two of these tablets tonight to help her sleep, and two three times each day after meals. She needs rest, healthy food and a lot of fresh air. Open the windows during the day,' he tell Mr Bopal. 'This place needs to be properly ventilated.'

Ma Bopal die two days after dat. Mai continue to work for Mr Bopal until he could get odder help. Besides, she didn't mind getting a few shillings for sheself. Two weeks later, Bopal bring Beepath, a old Hindu lady he say was family. So, Mai and Indrani stop working for Bopal.

One day, Mai say she meet Mr Bopal in Khalim's Uncle Sayeed's shop and when she was leaving home he say he could drop she home in de cart. Mai say she find dat strange. First time ever Bopal offer she a ride in de cart. But dat wasn't all. As soon as she get in de cart, he start up a conversation.

'Ma Khan,' he tell Mai, 'yuh know meh situation now. I is all alone since meh wife dead and ah want a wife.' Mai say she nearly burst out laughing, but on second t'ought she wonder why Bopal would want a wife she age. So, she t'ink again and realise dat maybe it was Indrani he was talking about.

He continue, 'I want to ask yuh about dis for some time now and ah glad ah see you dis morning, Ma Khan,' he pause. 'Ah want to get married to Indrani,' he say at last.

'What! How old you is Mister Bopal?' Mai didn't wait for de answer. 'My Indrani have only sixteen years. Yuh older dan she fadder, Mr Bopal, if he was alive!' she say.

'Ah sorry to take yuh by surprise, Ma Khan, but t'ink about it and tell me yuh answer later in de week.'

Mai say, when she step off de cart, she stand up for a while to steady she self and den, after a few minutes, she decide to go inside. When Mai relate de news to Indrani, she start crying right away.

'I tell yuh Mai, a long time now, I could feel he watching me in de corner of he eye. I know he didn't care about Ma Bopal. Mai, he not a good man,' she say to Mai.

'Beti, dohn say dat. He say he lonely and he want company. Look at de good side of t'ings and see what yuh could get for yuhself. Yuh dohn have no fadder and I old already. Bhai done leave home and Beta is only t'irteen years; he still a chile, poor boy. But he does do more dan enough. Bopal cyah live longer dan you. One day, yuh go be rich and all yuh troubles go be over,' she tell Indrani, trying to look on de bright side of t'ings.

'Mai, what I go do wit' a old man like dat – catch he dribble? I sure I go soon have to start minding him,' she tell Mai. Poor Indrani see living hell dat week. Mai say she used to have nightmares when she was sleeping and she used to wake up Mai sometimes during de night. When Mai tell Khalim's Auntie Deedee what happen, Khalim's Auntie say dey must go to de Mosque to pray. Besides, Bopal was a Hindu and he not religious anyhow – so dat make matters a little worse. Mai, Indrani and Khalim's Auntie start to spend more time togedder, and since I had leave de work on Mr Bopal land, I decide to ask for a work in de factory. In de next week or two, de factory would want help to manure all de cane land before planting new cane.

'Mai, yuh t'ink ah could pass for fifteen years?' I ask Mai.

'Yuh really brave, yuh know. Yuh is only t'irteen years now – wait 'till nex' year, nah!' she say.

'I dohn have much to do now, and yuh go want extra money for de wedding, too. Leh me try meh luck and see. De pay good, Mai, five shillings a week. Dat is a fortune – look, Bhai only getting two dollars a mont'!'

'Yuh know, Beta, in spite of all de falling out – if Indrani really getting married – we go have to tell Bhai. He mus' come to de wedding,' she say.

Mai and Khalim's Auntie Deedee plan de whole wedding togedder. Mai went to see Bopal two times again and dey decide on a date for de wedding. Mai

send me to tell Bhai dat he must take part in de ceremony and take Baap place, and be in charge o' Indrani
in case anyt'ing go wrong. Khalim's Uncle Sayeed offer
to take Baap place, but Mai say dat he wasn't Indrani's
flesh and blood. Bhai was so busy wid his own life, he
was so surprise when I give him de news.

'Indrani getting married to Bopal!' he shout. When
he get over de shock, at last, he say, 'A real blessing for
Mai, Beta – and Indrani too. You know Indrani older
than the two of us. She is sixteen years now and she
could pass for much more than sixteen. You, Beta, and
Indrani take by Baap's side. Look at you, taller than me
now. Both of you leave me close to the ground – I
come out short like Mai,' Bhai say.

'And guess what, Bhai?' I couldn't wait to tell him
about my luck. 'I get work in de Usine factory to
manure de cane land – five shillings a week!'

'What! a little boy like you!' he cried.

'Dat's what yuh t'ink. I pass for fifteen years; I is a
big man now, Bhai!' I tell him.

Anyway, Mai say dat Indrani wedding go be really
different from de usual Muslim wedding. First of all,
de *dulaha* is a Hindu and a old man, and de *dulahin* is a
Muslim wit' one brother, one sister and a mother – no
fadder. Khalim's Auntie Deedee and Indrani went to
San Fernando to buy material for Indrani's sari and veil
and pretty slippers, but Mai say she go buy her t'ings
right in Princes Town. She feel comfortable shopping
right here. Is too much trouble to go to High Street –
people staring at yuh and de police asking for yuh pass.

Bopal build two big tents outside in de yard and
invite nearly de whole village. A *pundit* say Hindu

prayers and Khalim's uncle on his mudder's side, Imam Ali, say Muslim prayers. Mai kill a goat and a sheep, and she and Khalim's Auntie Deedee was in charge o' de cooking. But, some of de women from de village do most of de work. Bhai and Gopee and Jai, Mai, me and de Hosein family stand on Indrani's side.

Indrani give a big smile dat day when Khalim's Auntie Deedee whisper to her, 'We always here for yuh chile, right here if yuh need we.'

One evening after we had finish eating, Mai was talking about Indrani wedding and one t'ing lead to de next. She take me by surprise when she start to talk about meh own life.

'Is nearly time for yuh to get married, too, Beta – look at you!' she say. 'All meh food dat yuh eating making yuh grow so big. Yuh know, Bhai resemble yuh father. But yuh walk and act more like yuh Baap, and yuh strong like him too. Yuh remember him, Beta? How he used to work high up in Maracas hills in de cocoa and coffee plantation?'

She was ready to start dreaming about de past, so I break de spell and say, 'Talking about cocoa, Mai, what about if we start growing some cocoa? Bhai say now dat is only two o' we in dis house, we could start selling vegetables in de San Fernando market. Mai, I have enough money to get a donkey and a cart. We cyah sell not'ing in Princes Town; people already have plenty food!'

'And cocoa, too?' Mai ask me. 'We dohn have enough land for dat.'

'Dohn worry, Mai. It will take some time for de trees to grow and bear plenty cocoa. But in de meantime, we could make cocoa stick and sell in de market – wit' other t'ings too.'

'Yuh see, Beta – yuh go be a rich man. Yuh mind fix on making money, plenty money,' she say, pointing a finger at me.

'Dat's a good t'ing, Mai. Yuh not complaining doh?' I say.

'Oh no! I not complaining; is time we should be doing better for we-self,' she say wit' a smile.

Me and Mai always talk about how worried we was about Bhai, it look like he know just what he want to do wit' his life.

Mai say, 'For a quiet child, he really grow up to be brave, to work with strangers – white people he know not'ing about.

'But Mai,' I tell she. 'Bhai is not de only Indian in de church, yuh know. Jai and Gopee in de church too and dey teaching little Indian children, just like Bhai. Dese boys dohn have to work de land like me. Dere work is to talk de whole day and learn from books, but yuh could only do dat if yuh have brains,' I say.

'I know he is a smart boy, Beta, but he not working for no money to talk about. How much you say de Reverend paying him – two dollars a mont'?'

'Well, Mai, dat is true but yuh never have everyt'ing in life. Besides dat, Bhai look like a happy man,' I say.

Bhai finish training as a teacher and now de church send him to teach in de Vistabella School. I dohn know exactly where dat is, but Bhai say is like when yuh leaving San Fernando and going to Port of Spain side, up north. He was livin' near de school with some odder teachers since Jai get transfer to Grant school and Gopee gone to de school in Couva.

'And yuh still cookin' for yuhself?' I ask him.

'Ah! that will soon change, Beta,' he say wit' a smile.

'W'at, yuh have a cook now, Bhai?' I ask him.

'No, I going to get engaged later this year,' he say. His whole face light up as he talkin'.'

'Engaged?' I ask. 'W'at's dat?'

'That is when the girl's family say is okay for you to visit her at the family house and you have to buy a ring for her,' he explain.

'Bhai, all o' dat go on and yuh dohn tell Mai?' I was so surprise, meh mout' fall open for a little while and I keep staring at him.

'I will tell Mai, but not yet; I just want to make sure everything will work out all right,' Bhai say. Den, Bhai explain to me how he meet dis lady he was talkin' about. He say sometimes he used to hold Sunday school class at de Susamachar Church and dat is where he meet dis lady. She used to come to collect she little brudder after Sunday school and he got a chance to talk to she. Sometimes, she would go to de church service afterwards wit' she whole family and he would say a few words to dem too. So, it look like Bhai was makin' a few friends for his own self for some time now.

Bhai used to go to school on Saturday also, to teach Bible class and meet de Reverend to talk about his work. After dat, he had a free half day, and so we would meet in de San Fernando market and we would ride in meh donkey cart and talk a long time like when we used to live in Maracas. Mai used to send some *roti* and curry for Bhai every Saturday, and I used to give him cocoa sticks to make tea, and cucumbers and tomatoes and anyt'ing we pick from de garden dat week.

One Saturday afternoon, Bhai and me leave de market and drive up a big hill and den down de hill on Keate Street, den turn de corner on Gordon Street. When we pass de corner Bhai say, 'Stop here, Beta; I want to show you something. You see that house up the road there, that is where my intended lady's family lives.'

'Yuh what?' I was confuse.

'The girl I want to get married to nah. That is where her family lives,' he say, pointing to a upstairs and downstairs house in de middle o' de town.

'And how yuh goin' to get inside dere, Bhai?' I ask him.

'All in good time,' he say wit' a dry smile on his face.

Mai say she t'ink it strange dat Indrani and Bopal married for a whole year and Indrani not even having a baby yet.

'What happen to all yuh?' Mai ask Indrani one day, when she had come to see how we was doing. 'It look like Bopal sleeping in de cane field, girl.'

'No, Mai,' Indrani cover she face with two hands because Mai make her feel shame.

'Come on, girl, yuh can tell yuh Mai everyt'ing. I is yuh best friend – dohn mind you married and all dat. Maybe Bopal have a problem. Remember dat Bopal first wife, Parbatee, didn't have one child. Indrani, yuh must tell Bopal to say prayers – dat man have to get a *pundit* to bless de house. He only t'inking about all different ways to make money. I does see him passing in de cart at five o'clock in de morning. What happen, bug bite him in de bed or what? Mohan say dat Bopal reach de cane field before everybody else to count every single ox cart dat carrying cane to de factory. Who does add up all dat money for him, Beti? I hope he does give yuh some. Yuh mus' tell him yuh want a dress, shoes and a chewry; and sign a paper and put yuh name on de land too,' Mai advise Indrani.

'He do dat already, Mai,' Indrani say.

'Yuh sure?' Mai ask.

'We went to de lawyer office in Princes Town and Bopal pay money to make a deed,' she tell Mai.

'Bopal can write, Beti?' Mai ask again.

'No Mai, but we print we finger mark on de paper. And de lawyer say to me dat I still young and I must learn to sign meh name because de English law in Trinidad dohn register dat me and Bopal married.'

Mai didn't understand. 'So if Bopal dead tomorrow what is yuh position?' Mai ask.

'I okay now Mai, since I put meh mark on de paper but not before dat, if Bopal was dead!' Indrani tell Mai.

'So Muslim and Hindu wife and children in real trouble in Trinidad and I dohn even know dat.' Mai shake she head. 'Beta, we go have to sign a paper too, and yuh have to learn to sign yuh name.' Mai spin 'round de room and walk back, facing me and Indrani. 'And yuh know somet'ing else – Bhai could teach yuh to read and write. He was right, yuh know, dis law could never outsmart Bhai,' she say.

Mai and Indrani start going to de mosque every Friday wit' Khalim's Auntie Deedee. Dey ask Khalim's uncle, de *imam*, to say special prayers for Indrani and Bopal during Ramadan mont'. Mai and Indrani spend de whole of *Eid* at Khalim's Uncle Sayeed's house – cooking and eating and praying and singing. All Khalim's family, friends and neighbours meet at dere house and de *imam* was dere too saying prayers. Mai bring home so much *roti* and curry, goat and *sawine*, I had to take some for Bhai.

De next morning after *Eid*, I went to work early and leave Mai still sleeping, but when I reach home about five o'clock in de evening, I see de back window was still shut. I notice dat Mai was lying on de bed and breat'ing hard and holding she chest. Right away, I jump in de donkey cart and went to find de doctor in Princes Town. I was able to get de same doctor who went to see Mr Bopal's first wife. Mai tell de doctor she chest was hurting and she couldn't breat'e. Dr Fenwick give Mai a injection and leave some medicine for her. De next day, Indrani stay with Mai and I went to bring Bhai home because Mai ask to see him.

'Yuh is a good chile, meh son,' she tell Bhai, 'and yuh have plenty sense. Yuh choose yuh own way and Beta choose he own; but remember, Beta go always be yuh brudder and Indrani go always be yuh sister. Always love yuh family. Yuh new religion dohn really matter. I understand what yuh trying to do, but remember what important is dat you mus' always live close to yuh brudder and sister. Remember how far we come from. Dis is a new land, a strange land and yuh must always help one anodder. Allah bless yuh meh children.'

Dat was de las' time Mai talk to any o'we. Mai die in she sleep. Indrani say she t'ink Mai was getting a stroke, but de doctor say it was a bad heart attack dat damage she lungs and weaken she body. Khalim's Auntie Deedee and de Hosein family help do everyt'ing for Mai's funeral. Bhai, me and Indrani was too shock to t'ink straight, let alone lif' a finger to do anyt'ing in de house. We bury Mai right in Princes Town. She would be happy to know dat she had a Muslim burial wit' Imam Ali to say prayers. It was jus' sad we couldn't bury she next to Baap – but we couldn't do not'ing to change dat.

Mai always used to say dat t'ree is a lucky number, but I disagree – dat number bring trouble for me and Indrani. After Mai pass away, Khalim's Nana die and before Khalim went back to Tunapuna, Mr Bopal pass away too. Mr Bopal was a Hindu, so we had to get a *pundit* to say de prayers and arrange to cremate him. De sea was too far away so we take him to de riverside and light de pyre dere. Indrani say she never know Bopal have so much family. Most of de mourners she see for de first time; one very old man say he was Bopal's uncle, one his cousin, and a next one say he was a 'in-law relative.' T'anks to Allah, nobody say Bopal was he father.

After de wake, plenty people ask Indrani to sell dem land. But Bhai say, 'Don't do anything yet; the price of land going up and besides that, you have to think about your future.'

Indrani was so confuse and scared to stay in Bopal's house alone after de funeral, dat I used to go and stay dere overnight. Bhai ask de Reverend to give him some time off from Bible study class over Easter holiday, so he could help out and spend time wit' we. Sometimes, when Khalim was visiting his Uncle Sayeed's family in Princes Town, Khalim would come over and it was like old times again – except dat we was all grown up.

'So what happening with you these days, Khalim?' Bhai ask him. We didn't see him for some time. He was a big man now, two years older dan Bhai. For de funeral, he was wearing a *kurta*, but whenever he travel down south he wear a shirt and pants. He was showing off a big moustache and short hair combed back, shiny wit' coconut oil. Indrani ask him, 'Yuh married yet, Khalim? No girls in yuh life yet?'

'Not yet, not yet girl; I too young for dat. Yuh see, Baap sick dese days, so I have to help him manage de shop. I used to carry de goods only, but now I really busy. Dese days, Baap forgetting where he put important papers and t'ings. Sometimes, his feet swell up so he cyah stand for long.' He seem worried about his Baap.

'Yuh Baap need a good rest, Khalim,' Indrani say. 'He work too hard for too long. Yuh dohn want to bring him dong here to spend some time? If he get away from Tunapuna, he could relax a little and ride around in yuh uncle's buggy and make friends wit' all de people in Princes Town.'

'I would like dat for Baap too, girl. But yuh know, Mai say one day she go wake up and find him dead in dat shop. He just not leaving home for anyt'ing. He is a slave to de business,' Khalim say.

When Khalim lef' Princes Town, Bhai tell Indrani is time to put she business in order. So he take we to a lawyer friend he know in de Christian church. Bhai say dat de lawyer used to help de Indians by telling dem how not to lose dere house and land. His name was Mr Patrick.

'He was a Hindu or a Muslim before he join de Church, Bhai?' I ask.

'I really don't know; his whole family is Christian, even his mother and father,' Bhai say. Bhai went on to say that Indians did come to Trinidad as far back as fifty years ago and Mr Patrick's family live more like de white man dan de Indian. Anyway, Bhai explain Indrani's position to Mr Patrick and he advise she to lease out de cane-land every year. In dat way, she could sell when de year was up or lease it out again if she wanted to keep it. She would have plenty time to decide what to do if she wasn't sure. Indrani was able to sign she name on de paper – t'anks to Bhai.

'There's another matter I want you to deal with,' Bhai say to de lawyer after he was finish wit' Indrani's business.

'And what's that, Sir?' de lawyer ask.

'I would like to change my name,' Bhai say. Indrani and me stare each other in de face, speechless.

'Write down your present name here on this sheet of paper and below here,' he point to a place lower dong on de paper, 'write your new name,' he tell Bhai. Bhai pause a little, take de paper and write Clarence Stephen Sanwar for de new name. At de bottom of de paper, Indrani and me sign as witnesses.

After we leave Mr Patrick's office, Bhai explain why he change his name. It had to do wit' a really bad experience he had when he went to look for work as a store clerk. Dat was before he had start working as a teacher in de Church school. Bhai say dat he had see de advertisement in de show window on High Street saying dat de store manager wanted somebody who could read, write and do Arit'metic. He had knock on de office door and went in, and come face to face wit' a lady sitting at a desk.

'The manager is busy now,' de secretary tell Bhai. 'You will have to wait for about half an hour.' She was what Bhai call 'coloured'. I not really sure what colour dat was; Bhai say she was mix wit' white and Negro, but she look closer to white. She was wearing a nice dress and face powder wit' a big bun on top o' she head and a ribbon tying de bun. Bhai say he sit down and wait for more like one hour, dan half an hour. Den, a white man in a white jacket and blue tie come out and ask, 'And where is Mr McKenzie?'

'Here I am, Sir. I am Mr McKenzie,' say Bhai.

'You're Mr McKenzie!' de store manager scream at Bhai. 'A little, insignificant, stupid coolie boy like you! Get out of my store and don't waste my time!' Bhai say dat de white man look really vex and spin around to go back in de office and slam de door behind him.

Bhai was teaching for ten years in Canaan, jus' a short distance from San Fernando, before de Reverend put him in charge of de Vistabella School. In Vistabella, de whole village was like a big cane-field and they use the school to give Bible lessons and hold Church service, too. It was a small school, but sometimes teachers had class outside, under de trees. Bhai also used to go to church on Coffee Street where he was baptise. He get to know plenty converts in de

Presbyterian religion who was living in San Fernando, and he used to teach dere children at Sunday School. Dey was all ages but sometimes de older children used to talk wit' him after class. Sometimes, after Church service he would come to see Indrani and me in Princes Town. But sometimes, a family would invite him for lunch.

One day de Aaron family invite Bhai for lunch and he was so excited. Bhai say Ma Aaron was a fat lady and she used to wear *orhni*, a veil in Hindu style, and leddar boots and Indian jewellery. But, de children used to wear western-style clothes and she daughters had hairstyles like de store manager's secretary. Bhai say dat she was a hard worker. He find out afterwards that she used to manage a shop dat her husband had, before he got kill by accident when somebody in de store, where he was working, fire a bullet by mistake. Mr Aaron was a bookkeeper and come to Trinidad before we was born. His family was living in Persia, but he had lef' home when he was a young man and live in India for some time before he decide to come here. He was Muslim, but change to de same religion like Bhai, only long before Bhai.

Bhai had his eyes on dese people's girl child for two years. In de meantime, he had save up some money and was looking for a piece o' land to buy in San Fernando. Indrani couldn't understand Bhai's reasoning.

'So, why he dohn just come to Princes Town and work and live here, and ask de Reverend to send him to dis school here. We have house and land – even if he want to build he own house – he go be comfortable here,' she tell me one day.

'Yuh dohn understand? Yuh is a big woman and married already, and yuh dohn know?' I tell she. 'Bhai buying land to get married and build a house in San Fernando. He want to live in de town and have a family in town. Bhai is not a cane-cutter, a buggy driver, or even a *sirdar*. Bhai is a Christian, a teacher and a town man, and Bhai want to get married to a girl from San Fernando.'

'Dat might be true, Beta; but with dat money he getting, he mightn't live long enough to raise a family!' she say looking very upset.

One Sunday afternoon when Bhai come home, he tell we about his plans. He had ask Ma Aaron if he could marry she youngest daughter.

'She is only seventeen years old, son; and when you get married where you going to live?' she ask Bhai.

'I have some money saved up, Ma Aaron, to buy a house spot in San Fernando,' Bhai say.

'You have enough money to build a house too?' she ask him.

'Not yet Mai, but I will soon,' he answer.

Ma Aaron tell Bhai to wait for a while until she daughter is eighteen years. She say that she know a old Indian woman name Harangee who want to sell she property on Gordon Street. She, one of she sons and her daughter-in-law plan to move to Couva, where she daughter-in-law's family had buy land from de government to plant cocoa. Bhai say she had problems paying for de property in San Fernando and decide to sell out. Harangee was asking one hundred pounds for de spot. So Bhai and Ma Aaron went to see de plot of land and it was more dan wort' it. Bhai didn't have all dat money doh, so Ma Aaron put dong half and dey decide to buy it in Bhai name and her daughter name. Her daughter name was Ariana.

Bhai get married in March dat year and I wasn't surprise. I remember it was de middle o' crop time and a really busy time for de St Madeleine sugar factory and de factory workers in Princes Town. It was a Saturday, and me and Indrani went to Bhai wedding in de Susamachar Church. It wasn't such a big wedding but at least we did know some people. Gopee and Jai, Khalim and Khalim's Auntie Deedee went too. Bhai tell us to sit close to de front behind him because we was his only guests. I suppose all de odder people at de wedding come from Bhai's wife side. Bhai was all dress up – white man style – in white, long-sleeve shirt, jacket and inside jacket wit' a chain, bow tie and long pants and shiny shoes. Bhai's bride had a long veil and long white dress wit' long sleeves, and she had gold earrings wit' a long, gold chain. She had a bunch o' roses too. After de church ceremony, a man take photographs and we follow de guests' buggies in Khalim's Uncle Sayeed's buggy to Ma Aaron's house for lunch. Khalim was driving de buggy. De white Reverend was dere too. After a while Khalim, Khalim's Auntie, Gopee and Jai went home. I t'ink it was because dey didn't really feel too comfortable wit' Bhai's new family and strange-looking Indians, but me and Indrani feel we had to be dere for Bhai. To me, Bhai was really brave to take such a big step. I wonder if he did know what he was getting into. To me, he look like he was de odd one out in de whole group of people in dat wedding. I start to feel so sad and lonely for Bhai. It look like he was about to enter a strange place wit' people he never see before, not knowing what going to happen to him next. For me, I was looking at a new place and people I never see or meet before. Aldoh dey was looking like me and Indrani, like dey come from India, dey was behaving like white people. All de same, Bhai was happy and excited about everyt'ing. It make me sad too to see he was still so young, and dat Baap and Mai couldn't be dere for him. Bhai was in de middle of a big lifetime adventure; and me and Indrani stand back and watch him in de same room, like he was in a different world from us.

Some people, including Bhai, make short speeches and dey wish de bride and groom healt', wealt', happiness and a big family. Me and Indrani had somet'ing to eat and drink. Dere was a lot of clatter wit' plates and glasses and de silvers. When de crowd break up in small groups and start to talk to dere friends, we move towards de veranda to a quiet corner, away from dem. We stand dere watching all dere movements and saying not'ing to one anodder for a little time. Bhai and his wife was sitting close to a table wit' a big cake and bottles of drink and plenty glasses. On one side o' table was a pile of presents people had bring for Bhai and his wife. Guests was going up to dem and shaking Bhai hand and kissing his wife. Me and Indrani wait for a time when dey was alone for a while, den we walk up towards dem. When Bhai see us coming, he stand up and reach out for me and we hug one anodder. Indrani kiss Bhai wife and I shake she hand. Den, Bhai introduce his wife to us.

'This is my brother, Manwar, and my sister,

Indrani, Ariana,' he say. She stand up and smile, and turn 'round and call to a young lady, who was standing near de table.

'Alice,' she say, 'ask Ma to come and meet Clarence's family: I'm so happy to meet you,' she say to we, still smiling. 'Where are the others?' she ask.

'Oh dey had to leave,' Indrani answer. 'Khalim's Auntie had to take de buggy back home early today for Khalim's uncle to use.' Indrani try to make a excuse for Khalim's family leaving de wedding so early.

'They left already!' say Bhai.

He look disappointed, but Ma Aaron soon come up to us and shake we hands, and say, 'I hope you are enjoying yourselves; you had something to eat and drink?' she ask. She turn to Bhai and say, 'You and Anna will soon be cutting the cake and then all the guests will have some.' Den, she ask to be excuse and went to talk to some more people.

Me and Indrani invite we new *bhowji* to come and visit Princes Town after she and Bhai settle down. Bhai's wife say dat she would like dat and promise to visit soon. After we had a bellyful of cake and some more to drink, we notice dat some people was beginning to move towards de front veranda o' de house, near de stairs.

'Time for we to go, Beta,' Indrani whisper to me. 'Bhai know where to find we if he want anyt'ing.' We say a quick goodbye to Bhai and we new *bhowji*, and head for home.

Now dat we had to start all over again, wit'out Mai and Bopal and Bhai, Indrani say she want to start a farm sellin' sheep and goats, chicken and eggs. She had always like animals and still remember de two goats Mai had leave with Khalim's mudder in Tunapuna, when we was moving down South.

'Bopal didn't want to mind animals except horses. He used to say dey make too much noise and mess up de place,' Indrani say. 'But de trut' is he didn't have time for dat; he was too busy with de cane and keeping track of de money he was making everyday.'

'I dohn mind cutting cane for de factory when t'ings bad, girl, but right now money not in de cane business. Yuh dohn see all dem South farmers planting cocoa? People have to look 'round and see how dey could make a living,' I tell Indrani.

'But de factory still making sugar. Mohan say dat Trinidad sugar going to America now, not England,' she say to me.

'How Mohan know dat?' I ask.

'Yuh remember Will, de boy we meet at de train station when we went to see Bhai in Canaan and Mohan give him a ride back here?' she say.

'Oh yes, Will, and he say his grandpappy give him dat big name!' I say, wit' a smile.

'Well, Will's fadder growing cocoa and when he carry it to de cocoa centre, and ask de people who packing it, dey say all de sugar and cocoa from dese islands going to America,' Indrani inform me.

'Well, girl, I dohn know where dat is, but I going to plant cocoa on Mai land,' I tell she.

De first t'ing I decide to do was to fix up de vegetables and keep dem going, because dat was food for me and Indrani. Den, I plan to ask Mohan to go to Lengua wit' me to buy some cocoa plants from his family and see how dey managing de whole business. Some farmers had stop working in de factory in Saint Madeleine in Princes Town to work in de oil field in Point Fortin; but I still want to plant cocoa, and de government actually send people 'round de island to tell farmers how to plant it.

Bhai was doing well for hisself. When next me and Indrani went to see him, we *bhowji* was having a second baby. Dere first child was a boy name James Scott – after his wife's fadder. Bhai's wife used to speak only English; she didn't understand Urdu and Hindi, but Bhai say sometimes he and his mother-in-law used to speak Hindi. When dey was alone, and when she was talking to she Indian friends, she used to speak in Hindi if dey couldn't speak English. Bhai's wife had two sisters. One was living on de same Street as dem, was married and belong to de Christian church – so Bhai had family in San Fernando to keep him happy. By de time de first big war had start abroad, Bhai had five children. Dey was all going to de school where Bhai was teaching in Vistabella and he wife used to stay home and look after de children.

Bhai still used to go to de market every Saturday, after he was finish teaching his Bible class at school. By dat time, de market wasn't too busy so we could talk, and Bhai would greet his friends in de old Indian way saying 'Salaam.' He used to teach some o' de Indian vendors' children and dey used to show great respect for him. Dey would always give him fruit and vegetables, and sometimes, when I was ready to leave market early, Bhai would ride in de cart wit' me until we reach his house. Sometimes, Indrani would send eggs, a chicken and *roti* for him. Bhai never like eggs too much, but he say his wife use dem to make cake and fancy food. He say she had a cook who use to work for some white people before, and she used to bake in de brick oven in de yard at his home.

One day, me and Indrani invite Bhai to come up to Princes Town and bring de children and his wife. Indrani was so excited, she make plenty Indian sweets – *kurma* and *mithai*, *jelaby* and *goolab jamoon* – de day before, and get up five o'clock dat morning to cook food. I help her cut up de chicken and clean de *bhagi* den went to meet Bhai at de train station. I wait in de cart for a short time, den de train come. Bhai and t'ree children get off de train.

'Where yuh wife, Bhai?' I ask him.

'Oh, she couldn't come, Beta; she stayed home with the baby,' he explain.

'And what about yuh second girl?' I ask him. I couldn't remember she name.

'She wasn't too well this morning,' Bhai say. 'She has a cold.'

'Well, lemme see if I could remember. Dis Beta name is James, dis Beti is Lily and dis Beta is Ben – dat is right?' I ask.

'Yes, Uncle,' dey say all togedder.

'Good! Well, is time to get in de cart for a ride! Yuh Auntie must be waiting for yuh,' I say, lif'ing de little girl first. When we reach de house, Indrani was so happy to see Bhai, dat she hug and kiss him, and dance 'round him like she was a little girl again. She spin him 'round like he was a partner on stage in a dance show. De children laugh and clap dere hands. Den, I introduce each one of dem to Indrani. She kiss and hug each child, and as we sit down to talk, de children lef' de room and run downstairs to play under de house.

'So what is the special occasion?' Bhai ask me and Indrani.

'Is *Divali*, Bhai,' Indrani answer. 'And de whole village celebrating, Hindus and Muslims, and everybody else. I want yuh children to see de *dyahs* when dey light up and what it is like in Princes Town for *Divali*; besides, yuh so busy. Is a long time since I see yuh.'

'You welcome to come to my house anytime,' Bhai say. 'Why you don't come to San Fernando to see the stores, now that you making so much money selling animals and all,' he say to Indrani.

'Is not de same like when yuh come here, Bhai. It feel like home when yuh here and yuh bring all de old memories wit' yuh – like when we use to live in Maracas,' she answer him, wit' chin cup in hand and eyes welling up wit' water. I was sure she was going to cry as de memories start to flow.

'I didn't know yuh ask Bhai to come here to talk,' I butt in. 'Where de food, girl? We hungry!' She get up as soon as I say dat and start dishing out de food. I was helping to carry de full bowls and plates to de table, when a song start up down below. We stop what we was doing and run down de steps to see what was happening. Bhai's children was running 'round and 'round de animals, singing as loud as dey could:

Old Mac Donald had a farm and E, I, E, I,
O

And on this farm he had some goats and E,
    I, E, I, O
And a meh! meh! here...

Bhai and me burst out laughing, and Indrani ask, 'Who is old Mac Donald?'

After lunch, I take Bhai and de children to see meh garden and meh cocoa field. De garden was in tip-top shape, but de cocoa trees was still young. Some of dem had only small pods, but de plants look green and healt'y. I used to water dem everyday and pull out de weeds whenever dey start to grow tall. I had plant four mango trees to mark de boundaries of Mai's land and one of dem was already bearing fruit. So I pick some and put in de cart for Bhai's children, and collect some string beans and pull out two *cassava* for Bhai.

'Yuh plant anyt'ing on yuh land, Bhai?' I ask him. 'Yuh have a big yard, you know!'

'Oh, yes,' he say. 'When a baby born in my family, I plant a fruit tree. So I have five fruit trees – one mango, one cherry, one pommerac, a coconut and a pommecythere tree.'

'And how many more trees yuh going to plant, Bhai?' I ask him.

'You playing smart, eh?' he smile. 'Maybe about two or three more – we could do with a guava tree, another coconut and a pawpaw,' he say, trying to imagine what de complete yard would look like. We was walking towards de back o' de land, when Bhai notice a change. He turn 'round to take a second look at de yard. He notice dat I had break down de old carat house we used to live in and start to dig out holes to put wooden posts in.

'And what you doing here?' Bhai ask me.

'Ah building a house – a wooden one dis time, and in de back I making a big space to dry out de cocoa. Just now I go be a cocoa farmer, Bhai, not just a market vendor. How yuh like it?' I was hoping de change would please him.

'Good work, Beta, I am really proud of you. You always liked to work in Baap's garden, I remember. And all this hard work you put in here… at last, you're seeing your way,' he say as he pat me on meh shoulder.

After we drive back to de house in de cart, I find dat de children was looking a little tired from playing in de hot sun. De younger boy, Ben, was ready to bite a mango, but Bhai tell him, 'Don't eat that yet, son; we're taking them home. You may soil your clothes and that means more work for your Ma. Besides, we have to keep a mango for Ma and one for Rose.'

When we reach back to de house, Indrani give de children somet'ing to drink and dish out small cups of *goolab jamoon* for Bhai and de children.

'What's this, Pa?' Lily ask Bhai.

'*Goolab jamoon*, it's nice,' say Bhai. Taste the syrup first.'

'Mmmm – sweet, can Ma make this?' she ask.

'I don't think so,' Bhai answer, 'so eat it all up.'

Bhai say it was getting late and dey had to leave to get de train back to San Fernando. So Indrani wrap up some sweets for de children and kiss all o' dem, and I drive dem and Bhai back to de train station.

Indrani used to spend most of de day looking after de sheep and goats – dey was still young, but de chickens was growing fast and laying eggs. She had plant some corn for dem and use to pound it in a mortar to grind it up. When she had a good amount of eggs, she used to ask Khalim's Uncle Sayeed to sell dem in de shop for she. Sales wasn't too good because most people in de village didn't use eggs. But when I take dem to San Fernando market on Saturday, dey sell out fast. So Indrani used to make plenty money at certain times o' de year. When it was *Divali* or *Eid*, or dere was a wedding in de village, or special prayers for feeding de poor, de animals would sell too.

One Saturday before Christmas, Bhai come to de San Fernando market and tell me his wife's family want some meat for de season, but dohn want de trouble to kill and clean de animals. I ask Bhai if dey want eggs too, because town people was mostly Christians and dey used to eat different from we. Bhai say he was sure to get some orders for Indrani, and it was a pity cocoa didn't sell for Christmas, too. So me and Indrani get smart and ask Bhai to help we find customers in town for goat meat, lamb and eggs. If we could do dat business a few times in de year, I could make enough money to plant more cocoa and den finish build meh house by de end of de next crop time.

One day when I reach home, I meet Indrani wrapping up she money in a old towel and tying a knot with de two ends.

'What yuh doing, girl?' I ask she.

'I just trying to hide meh money when yuh come, Beta,' she say, smiling. She put de towel in a big pot, cover de pot and push it under de bed.

'Yuh know Indrani, dat is not a good place to keep money. Is true we never had money before, but we must ask Bhai how to put it in de bank,' I tell her.

'Yuh think it safe in de bank?' she ask. 'Khalim's uncle say is only white people working in de bank. I dohn t'ink I really trust dem wit' meh money, Beta.' She look really worried about de problem.

'All right, next time I see Bhai, I go ask him if yuh should keep dat money under de bed or put it in de bank, and if dey will let yuh put it in de bank,' I tell she.

De next time I see Bhai in de market, I ask him about de bank business.

'You must have a birth certificate,' Bhai tell me. 'And be able to sign your name and count your money, if you want to put money in the bank.'

'What is dat – birth certificate?' I ask Bhai. I was confuse.

'That is a paper from the country you were born in, saying what day and year you were born and what place you were born in,' he explain.

'And how I go get dat, Bhai?' I ask him.

'We have to go to the lawyer again and make a paper for you,' he say.

'And Indrani, too,' I remind him.

'Indrani must get somebody older than her to go to the lawyer to sign the paper, somebody who can read and write,' he continue.

'And why you cyah do dat?' I didn't believe Bhai wasn't good enough. After all, he was a schoolmaster.

'I can't sign a paper to say I know when Indrani was born, Beta, because Indrani is older than me.' I started to t'ink about what Bhai was saying.

'So maybe we can ask Khalim's Auntie Deedee, den?' I say.

Bhai shake his head, 'No, I think Khalim's uncle might be better; you see, Beta, the business is in Khalim's uncle's name and that means he is respected in Princes Town. Besides which, I don't think Khalim's Auntie can read and write.'

'So you have to be a man, and a rich one at dat, to sign a paper den, eh Bhai?' I was getting more confuse.

'To be rich is good, but to help yourself, you must be able to read and write and count – especially your own money,' Bhai advise me.

So Bhai, me and Indrani went back to Bhai's lawyer friend – and Khalim's Uncle Sayeed had to go, too – to get a birth certificate so we could put we own money in de bank. Bhai advise Indrani to come to San Fernando sometimes and visit de stores so she could know de value of she money – how much different t'ings cost. Now dat a few Indians had stores on High Street, she shouldn't feel so bad; she could speak a little Hindi or Urdu, depending on who de store owner is.

'Dat is true, Bhai?' she ask him.

'Oh yes. There's Rahamut – selling cloth and shoes for men and women. And Bunsee sells all Indian foodstuff and kitchen utensils – like pots and pans, and enamel plates. There's a jewellery store too, called Sultan Khan,' Bhai tell Indrani.

'Sorry, Bhai, but I not ready to walk in High Street. Yuh know what I t'ink? I should tell Gopee or Jai dat I want to come to school because I want to write meh own name, Indrani Bopal.' So Indrani had make de decision to 'become educated,' as Bhai put it.

Indrani say she find it strange she didn't see

Khalim's Auntie Deedee for a few weeks and wanted to go to see if she was sick. One evening, we went to see she and de Hosein family. As we was walking in de yard, we meet Nat', Khalim's Auntie son and he was just coming from school. He was going to a secondary school in San Fernando dat Bhai wanted his sons to go to – but Nat' was Muslim – and before dat he used to go to de Christian school in Princes Town when he was small. He was a smart boy and could speak English like Bhai, but didn't speak Hindi or Urdu. Khalim's Auntie Deedee say dat sometimes Nat' used to invite some of his Christian friends home. She didn't mind dat as long as he keep his own name and religion, and not change it like dem.

'So, you two Muslims, dohn go to de Mosque again?' Khalim's Auntie Deedee ask me and Indrani. I didn't know what to say, and Indrani hide she face behind she *ohrni*.

'We didn't go for a long time; sometimes, we so busy we just forget all about de Mosque,' Indrani say.

'Dat not good enough,' Khalim Auntie say. 'Starting next Friday, you and Indrani come meet me and we can go togedder like a family. I know yuh Mai was a religious woman and she wouldn't like if yuh stop praying in de Mosque. After *Ramadan*, I planning to invite all de Muslims in de village to have prayers and feed de poor. De way t'ings going, I dohn know how long I have to live; dese days, I dohn feel too good, chile.'

After *Ramadan*, Indrani and me spend *Eid* wit' Khalim's Uncle Sayeed and de family. Khalim's uncle, de *imam*, say prayers and afterwards, we sing and eat, and meet some Muslims we didn't know before. Khalim's Auntie make sure she introduce me and Indrani to everybody. Indrani went to help in de kitchen, but Khalim's Auntie tell Nat' to introduce me to de nice young ladies sitting in a corner and hiding behind each odder. One of dem was braver dan de rest and ask me meh name and where I live. She say she used to see Indrani come to school in de evening class, but never speak to she.

'An' yuh go to dat school?' I ask.

'Yes, and my friends here, too, Indra and Rema. My name is Saleema, Saleema Mohammed. We live close to de town. My Baap is a jeweller – you know where?' she ask me.

'No, but when I want to buy jewellery, I know where to go now,' I say smiling. She say she Baap wanted she to learn how to read and write, and not to change to a Christian. But, de Reverend in de school was always trying to tell dem about de new religion. Den, I tell she about Bhai and how he join de Christian church and is a teacher living in San Fernando.

'And your Baap let him do dat?' she ask.

'Baap die a long time ago, when we was living in Maracas,' I say. I couldn't remember exactly how long ago.

'Oh, sorry to hear dat,' she say in a soft voice.

Indrani continue going to school and when we had time in de evening, she show me how to read and write and count a little. But I could never do such t'ings as good as Indrani. Anyway, I learn to count my money, so de officer at de cocoa centre could never cheat me when I sell meh cocoa.

One morning, I take t'ree bags of cocoa to de centre and I notice dey had change up de clerks. When de clerk write down de amount of bags and how much money I had to get paid, I had to take de paper to de cage and sign meh name to collect meh money. As I shift de paper to sign, I look at de clerk. Somewhere, I was sure I see dat face before. I continue to write, taking meh time.

'Manwar – that is you?' I hear somebody say to me. When I look up, I see de clerk wit' a puzzle look on he face.

'Yes – and who is dis?' I question de young man dat keep looking at me.

'Will – William Fowell,' he say, waiting for me to recognise him.

'Oh yes,' I cut him short. 'De boy with de big name! So yuh have big work, Will – dat's good. I never see yuh here before. Yuh going to keep dis work?' I ask.

'Oh yes, I think so. I working here only one week now,' he say.

'Well, is good to know somebody in here, Will,' I say. 'I hope to see yuh next time I come.'

When I get meh cocoa money, I decide to buy something nice for Indrani in San Fernando. I look 'round de town a little and see some jewellery in a store. I t'ought maybe I could buy something small – not too dear. But, it might be better to buy it in Princes Town – from Saleema's fadder. How come I didn't t'ink of dat before? Den, as Bhai say, I could 'kill two birds wit' one stone'. So, I went back to de station and take de train to Princes Town.

It was early in de afternoon – maybe a bad time to visit, but dis was really a business visit. Saleema's fadder had a shop at de back of de house; but as de back door was shut, I walk 'round de front. I could hear somebody sweeping.

'*Salaam, salaam*,' I call. I hear footsteps coming.

'Oh, is you, Manwar,' say Saleema.

'Who is dat?' a older voice ask.

'Mai, is Manwar – you remember we meet him by Nat's Baap house for *Eid*,' Saleema explain. Saleema's mother stare at me wit' a puzzle look on she face.

'Oh, yes, Manwar. Yuh want somet'ing in de shop? I see yuh coming 'round from de back. We close de shop at lunchtime and open again in de afternoon. Hardly anybody does come during lunchtime,' she say.

'I sorry to disturb yuh, Ma Mohammed,' I say. 'I could come back anodder time if yuh busy.'

'No, no, come inside. It look as doh yuh a little tired – sit down,' she say pointing to a chair.

'I just come back from San Fernando; dis morning, I sell t'ree bags of cocoa,' I say, stressing de 't'ree.'

'Dat's good,' she answer, smiling. 'I see yuh is a hardworking man.' She turn to Saleema and tell she, 'Bring some water for Manwar to drink. I sure he t'irsty. So you want somet'ing from de shop?' she ask me a second time.

'Yes. I want to buy a small present for meh sister, Indrani,' I say.

'Yuh want Saleema's fadder to make somet'ing for yuh? Yuh have gold or yuh want what he make already?' she ask me.

'I dohn have any gold,' I mutter.

'I can open de shop for yuh to see what he have dere – leh me get de key.' She move 'round de room and fumble in a drawer for de key. In de meantime, Saleema give me a cup of water.

'Sal, see if yuh fadder wake up yet!' she call to Saleema. Somehow, I had de feeling she didn't want Saleema close by me, so I drink de water, put de cup on de table and walk to de door. Den, Saleema's fadder enter de room.

'*Salaam, salaam,*' I say and bow to him. 'I sorry to trouble yuh, Mr Mohammed.'

'No trouble, no trouble at all,' he answer. 'Leh me open de door for yuh. I dohn have too many t'ings now – business quiet dese days, but if is somet'ing small, yuh lucky. Yuh see, people like to bring dere own gold most times for me to make it over. Dis is what I have here.' He climb on a bench, run his hands along a high shelf and lif' up a blue leddar case. He rest it on de counter, unlock it and raise de cover. He take out several gold rings, one at a time, and look at each one. He show it to me and put it back in de case.

'How much for one ring?' I ask.

'Each of dese is twenty shillings,' he reply.

'And de nose ring?' I ask again.

'Ten shillings and eight pence for de smaller ones,' he say.

'I like dis one wit' de red stone,' I say. He take dat one out o' de case again and place it on de counter for me to examine.

'Yuh taking it?' he ask.

'Yes, I like dis one,' I decide, after holding it in meh hand and looking at it again. He wrap it in a small piece o' white paper and hand it to me. I roll out ten silver shillings and eight big brown pennies from a long piece o' cotton I had tie around meh waist and line dem up on de counter to make sure I had de exact amount o' money.

'Sal,' Mr Mohammed call his daughter. 'Come a minute!' he shout. He turn 'round to face she and whisper somet'ing. She look at de ten shillings and de eight pennies. She nod she head, den collect dem one by one, dropping each coin in a brown velvet drawstring purse. I put de jewellery in meh pocket, bow and say 'Salaam' before leaving.

When I unwrap de nose ring and show it to Indrani, she exclaim, 'Beta, I really like it! And wit' a little red stone too! Who choose it for yuh?' Indrani ask.

'So what yuh saying, I dohn have taste?' I ask she.

'No, no, Beta. I dohn mean dat! How much yuh pay for dis?' she ask.

'Yuh not to ask dat – is a present for yuh. So much work yuh doing everyday and not buying anyt'ing for yuhself. When yuh going out, yuh must look nice, odderwise people might t'ink yuh working on de estate,' I say.

'T'anks Beta, yuh is really a good brudder,' she say, smiling more dan ever, and she give me a hug and a tight squeeze 'round meh neck as if she want to choke me.

Indrani say dat she meet Gopee in Princes Town market and he say Bhai tell him dey had a next baby, a girl.

'Anodder baby! So how many children dat make?' I ask her. 'Now girl, you t'ink Bhai could mind all dose children?' I couldn't believe meh ears.

'Dat make six now, t'ree boys and t'ree girls. Bhai rich in his own way – poor people riches! He must spend all de money he work for in food,' Indrani say.

'Well, de last time I see him he say he buy a cow and de boys old enough to look after it, so dey have enough milk. But imagine feeding all dose children. I hope Bhai know what he doing. I hope he can manage,' I say.

'And Beta, if yuh see dem, all of dem fat and have good size. Yuh know all dere names, Beta?' she ask me.

'No, not all o' dem,' I answer. 'Yuh remember when dey did come here and was dancing 'round de animals and de little girl, Lily, she like de *goolab jamoon*? And de big boy was quiet, but de little one was troublesome?' I remind she.

'Beta, yuh know somet'ing? I t'ink we should go and see Bhai – maybe we could take a few t'ings for him and de family,' she suggest.

'And we *bhowji*, too?' I tease she.

'Why not? Maybe she not be too nice to we, but she not going to bite.' Indrani cup a hand over she mout' as if to hold back what she had already say.

De next Saturday after lunch, me and Indrani pack up de donkey cart wit' everyt'ing we had to give Bhai and drive to San Fernando.

When we reach de house, one of Bhai's small children run outside in de road to see who it was, but he didn't recognise we and he went back in. Den, two of de older children come out, a girl and a boy. De girl was about eleven or twelve years old and de boy look younger.

'Good afternoon,' she say. 'You come to see Pa?'

'Yes,' Indrani answer. 'He home now? We bring a few t'ings for him. How de other children?'

'Oh, they are well!' she say, staring at us and trying to figure out who we was. When she recognise who we was, she say, 'Uncle Manwar, is that you? And Aunt Indrani!'

'Ben,' she say to de boy, 'go and tell Ma we have family visiting.' De little boy disappear towards de back o' de house and I say to she, 'Yuh mus' be Lily.'

'Oh yes, I am Lily.' She come closer and kiss me and Indrani, and hold we hands. 'Bring the donkey in the yard, Uncle, and tie the rope on to the fence. You drove him all the way from Princes Town?' she ask me. Den, de little boy come back and say somet'ing to Lily.

'Ben, this is Uncle Manwar and Aunt Indrani, don't you remember them?' Lily ask him. Ben wasn't sure, so she tell him to bring some water in de bucket for de donkey to drink. She lead us toward de house. De front door was lock from inside, so we pass 'round de back.

'Where yuh Mai, Lily?' I ask her.

'Oh, Ma is with the baby. She hasn't been very well and Pa went to his school at Vistabella to help transfer the furniture to the new building,' she explain. 'You know, his school now has about two hundred students and so Pa has more work to do.'

We were so taken by Lily and her nice ways, dat we forget everyt'ing in de cart until Ben recognise a bottle o' sweets Indrani make for de children. Den, we empty de cart and put everyt'ing on a big table in de dining room. Lily look at each bottle and open each parcel.

'And you brought all these for us – *kurma*, *jelaby*, *roti*, curried meat!' she exclaim. She look so happy and excited.

'Goat meat,' Indrani tell her.

'Two bottles of milk, tomatoes, *bodi*, mangoes, cocoa sticks, eggs and a hen,' she continue, talking out a list o' all the t'ings we bring.

'We have to tie de hen,' Indrani tell her. 'I have a string – just in case she want to run away as de place strange.'

'Don't worry, Auntie. Pa built a fowl coop, so I'll just close her up inside of it,' she say.

'Come, leh me carry it for yuh – show me where to put it,' I tell she. I t'row de hen in de bottom of a big chicken cage and latch de door. We go inside de house to de dining room and sit on a long bench on one side of a big table, and anodder bench was on de odder side.

'Where all de odder children?' I ask.

'Well, James and Rose went with Pa, and Cynthia went to church for her First Communion class. You want something to drink?' she ask me and Indrani.

'Some water,' I say.

'Me too,' say Indrani. Lily take down two glasses from a tall cabinet in de dining room and pour water from a clay gourd in dem. It was nice and cold. When we was finish drinking, she ask me and Indrani, 'Would you like to come to see Ma and the baby now?'

'Oh no, dat's all right. Just tell she we bring dis for everybody. Is time for we to leave before it get too late. We have to reach home before dark, yuh know,' Indrani say. Lily kiss we again and as we sit in de donkey cart and pull out de yard, Bhai come home wit' two of de older children. So, we meet Rose and James, and wave goodbye to Lily again.

In Princes Town, Jai and Gopee say dey went to Bhai's church on Coffee Street to celebrate a special occasion, de opening of Bhai's new school in Vistabella. 'The old school was more than twenty years old,' Gopee say, 'and next Saturday, Susamachar having a bazaar to raise funds to help make desks and benches for the school.'

'What is dat?' I ask Gopee.

'A bazaar? That is when people sell things for the Church to raise money. They get all the church members to give food, cakes and sweets, even fruits and vegetables, and all your friends can come and buy,' he explain.

'What yuh selling, Gopee?' I ask him.

'Who me? I not selling; I coming to buy and eat and enjoy myself, to see the children playing and all the young girls. Guess who coming, too?' he ask smiling. He touch me on meh shoulder, 'Saleema!' he shout.

'So de whole o' Princes Town coming too?' I ask.

'Not really, only if they get invited by the church members – so Manwar, you and Indrani must come to the bazaar. At least you will see Bhai and his wife and all the children, and you'll be able to spend a little time with them,' Gopee say.

Me and Indrani went to de bazaar. As usual, Indrani make a set of t'ings – not food dis time, but all kinds of sweets. I pack up de cart with coconuts, mangoes, tomatoes, salad beans, pumpkin, peppers and corn. When we was leaving, Indrani tell me, 'Dohn forget to carry a cutlass to cut de coconut and a knife, de basket of eggs and de cocoa sticks.'

Bhai was so surprise to see us when I pull up wit' de donkey cart full of t'ings. He couldn't believe how many different t'ings we bring to sell.

'Beta, you giving the church all of this! You sure you don't want to keep some?' he ask.

'Not for de church, Bhai, for yuh school. Gopee say yuh school need money to buy desks and benches for de children to use. Just make sure yuh school get de money and not de church,' I say.

Bhai get some of de teachers from his school to help empty de cart and put everyt'ing on some desks and benches dat dey had borrow from Grant School, de school next door, named after one of de missionaries in de Christian church. I lead de donkey in de shade and give it some water to drink. Bhai try to help some of de teachers to arrange de stalls, but dey tell him to take a break and enjoy hisself. So, we walk 'round de church grounds to see all de stalls, de people and de children enjoying demself. Some little children was playing a game, holding long ribbons, and dancing in and out around a tall bamboo pole. A white lady was in charge o' de game and she was playing music in a box. Bhai say dat was a gramophone. When I ask de lady what game de children was playing, she say, 'Oh, that's the Maypole dance, Sir. Would you like to join?'

I just smile and say, 'No, t'ank yuh, Ma'am.'

Bhai shake de lady's hand and bow. She say, 'Good morning, Mr Sanowar. I'm so excited about the Fair – I'm sure we'll do very well today. The turnout is very encouraging.'

'I pray we will do well, for the children's sake, Miss Hall,' Bhai answer. Then he turn to face me and say to her, 'This is my brother from Princes Town; he donated a huge cart full of foodstuff.' I see de lady's face light up.

'Oh thank you so much, Mr Sanowar,' she say, holding out her hand to shake mine. I was about to say dat my name was Mr Khan, but Bhai wink at me and tell she we want to walk 'round de church grounds.

Bhai say de teachers from his school and Grant School had do most of de work and sell everyt'ing. Dey bring *roti* with *talkari* – curry wrap inside, curry *channa*, *dhal* and rice, fried split pea pies and Indian sweets. De town Christians had more English-style t'ings selling like cakes, bread and pies, and 'sweets and candies imported from Canada and England,' Bhai say. Some stalls had vegetables, fruits, cocoyea brooms, straw mats, pencils, copybooks and slates for children to write on. One Canadian church lady was selling small toys and books wit' pictures for children. Bhai did know almost everybody and greet dem saying, 'Good morning' and '*Salaam*' too. People had dress in *dhotis* and *kurtas* and *ohrnis*; but de town people had shirts, ties and jackets. Some ladies was wearing hats for de hot sun while selling t'ings, but some just sit in de shade chatting and looking at everyt'ing. Bhai's wife was sitting wit' dem.

Indrani had disappear with some friends she know in Princes Town and went to evening class wit' at de school. It was not 'til later, dat me and Bhai happen to see she talking to Saleema. So, we walk up to dem and I introduce Bhai to Saleema.

'You enjoying yourselves ladies?' Bhai ask dem.

'Oh yes, Bhai, I really like dis bazaar. Look at what I buy, Beta – a picture for de house,' Indrani say, showing we a picture wit' two horses and a buggy, and a white man in a tall hat driving it. It look like de horses was running fast because de man was holding on to his hat and he look like he was falling over.

'Well, I see yuh want me to fall out de buggy, too, Indrani?' I ask her.

'Oh no, Beta!' she say and all of we just laugh.

By about four o'clock, most o' de food was finish and some people wit' little children was already leaving. Bhai was checkin' on his teachers to see if dey wanted help, and Indrani say it was time to go. She suggest we take some o' Bhai's children home so dey wouldn't have to walk. Bhai tell Lily and James, and two of de smallest children to come wit' me and Indrani. De odder children would walk and we bhowji would get a ride home wit' a church member. He would stay until all de desks was cleared and de churchyard was clean and tidy. So I give meh donkey some water and get him ready to leave. We pull out o' de churchyard and head for Gordon Street and den Princes Town.

CHAPTER 3

Family Blessings

God bless this home
When children's voices sing
And peals of laughter ring in
carefree joyousness;
When love fulfils the need
And comforts hearts that bleed
from worldly bitterness.
God bless this land
When kin and friend alike
In brotherhood unite, amidst
diversity.
May thanks and praise be given
For boundless gifts from Heaven
through all eternity.

A riana Sanowar was the third of four children. She had two elder sisters, Alice and Sarah, and one brother, Harvey. Like her siblings, Ariana belonged to that first generation of children born to immigrant families of the Caribbean. Her mother, however, was native to a region in north-western India, the foothills of the Baluchistan Mountains, overlooking the Indus River. It was a lush, green, sprawling countryside which she had treasured as a child. She recalled her father's memorable descriptions of his adolescent experiences, accompanying his father and other caravan traders across the treacherous mountain passes, bringing camels and horses from Kandahar to India. Sometimes, when they were lucky, they brought silk and wines, wool and leather, fruits and nuts, and a variety of medicinal herbs. Among the latter, asafoetida was most valuable. Mary Hari's father, Ben Al Hari, who was born in Multan, belonged to a family of traders, some of whom had crossed the western border and lived in Persia for decades. But, when the British seized control of all trading posts and seaports in that area the Kandahar marketplace ceased to exist. Both mercantile and land traders were forced to use British ships and British-controlled Indian ports to transport their merchandise. Frustrated by these restrictions necessary to continue his family occupation, Ben Al Hari decided to leave his family home and move south, closer to an environment that was more conducive to trading.

After much deliberation, Ben decided to set up a merchant's shop in Bombay. Under British control, the port had developed into a huge commercial entrepot. It was fed by a vast network of railways, which served to drain its hinterland, particularly of cotton. Indian cotton left the country in British ships for England, and Indian merchants travelled on British ships to sell their goods wherever the ships sailed. Throughout the East, Indian cotton was famous for its excellent quality and although Eastern merchants were still very interested in purchasing Indian cotton, this was forbidden by the British. Nevertheless, there were other kinds of merchandise Ben Al Hari could sell to India's neighbours. The railways facilitated the movement of traders in large numbers from the northern and eastern regions. Ben decided that he would open a market for the sale of expensive Kashmir garments, made from northern Indian wool. These were in great demand by the Persians. He would offer also a variety of spices and teas, some of which entered India's eastern ports from the Far East and were brought to Bombay by Indian and Chinese traders. The Eastern world created a huge market for spices, for both medicinal and religious purposes. This was especially true of the Persians, who had been India's largest trading partners for centuries. Their transhipment port of Bandar Abbas was leased to the rulers of Oman and this development brought greater opportunities for Persian traders to sail to neighbouring ports, including Bombay.

A few months after his relocation to Bombay, Ben Al Hari met two interesting visitors at his merchant shop. It was late afternoon when Ben Al Hari relieved his weary legs and sank into his comfortable, bamboo armchair. He sat back, watching the scorching sun creep slowly down the horizon behind a fleet of merchant ships anchored in the harbour. His assistant, Raj, was restocking the shelves with items that had been sold that day. He had just one chore left to complete, namely, packing a small box of items for Ben to take home before the cart driver arrived to meet them. Ben must have dozed off for a few minutes when he felt Raj touch him on his shoulder and say in the local Hindustani dialect, 'Sahib, two men here to see you; they look like visitors.'

'They are very late – too late to bargain a good price,' mumbled Ben, a bit disgruntled that his short slumber had been curtailed. He looked up and glimpsed two strange men standing in the doorway of his shop, one much older than the other. They were not Indians, but they were certainly Eastern. They wore white, tailored *kurtas* and simple, brown turbans. Their attire revealed that they were prepared for the hot Indian days. 'Bring them inside, Raj. I'm too tired to get up and move around,' he said.

'*Salaam, salaam,*' they both greeted Ben and bowed several times.

'We are traders from the Gulf region and this is our first visit to Bombay,' the older man said. 'This is my son, Ahruhn, and I am Nazir Ali Ahmed.'

He spoke in Urdu, a language Ben knew well. It was originally a camp dialect, the language of northern India, including his home district, and was used among former caravan traders who travelled to the western countries of the Afghans and the Persians. Ben was wearing the customary Muslim dress, garments similar to those of his visitors.

'Welcome to Bombay! I hope your voyage will be a fruitful one,' said Ben. 'Most shops are closing now or are already closed, but I trust tomorrow you will be able to purchase what you desire.'

'Certainly,' said the older gentleman. 'We are as tired as you are. Our merchandise will be brought to shore tomorrow morning. Now, we are seeking a certain place of rest. Do you know where this is?' he asked. He showed Ben an address written in a small leather-cased notebook. Ben recognised the address immediately.

'Oh, yes!' he exclaimed. 'Sahib Kublalsingh's lodging is on the road to my house. I can give you a ride as soon as the cart driver comes to meet me,' offered Ben.

'Thank you, thank you!' they uttered simultaneously. When the cart arrived, the four men quickly boarded and the horses headed for home.

The following morning, Sahib Ahmed and his son were waiting in front of Ben's shop when he arrived to begin the day's work.

What began as a meeting of coincidence developed into an enduring friendship. When Nazir Ali Ahmed fell ill and could no longer endure the ordeals of merchant voyages, Ahruhn took control of his father's business. He spent more time in Bombay and became Ben's business adviser. When his father died, he married Ben's daughter, Mary, and revealed to Ben his desire to travel to the New World, which he claimed was filled with promise and adventure. The Old World had already been conquered by the Europeans. It was time for him to move on and prove himself a successful businessman in a new environment. He knew there was a demand for all the requirements of a prosperous country – food and clothing, household utensils, domestic and garden tools, footwear, construction materials and equipment. He could visualise the needs of recently freed Africans and the deprived, struggling, indentured Indian labourers nostalgic for the culture of their homeland. He had access to merchants who could supply many needs of these immigrant peoples. Firstly, Ahruhn planned to work for one of the successful businessmen in the

British colony of Trinidad, until he was confident he could open his own enterprise. He decided that he and his wife would sail on the *Cochin*, a merchant vessel owned by Francisco da Souza, a Portuguese merchant from Goa. Da Souza had planned a long voyage and would set sail in the month of January, carefully avoiding the stormy weather. He intended to stop at four ports of call before he arrived at his final destination in the West Indies. After leaving Bombay, where Ahruhn and Mary would embark, he would stop at Bandar Abbas, Ahruhn's birthplace and family homeland. There he would sell most of the spices he acquired in India and purchase a quantity of Persian rugs, carpets, cotton and silk garments, as well as wine for the merchants of Muscat in Oman, his second stop. At his third stop in Delagoa Bay, Mozambique, they would be joined by two wealthy Portuguese business-men, who had travelled to the West Indies and had relatives who were living in Trinidad. Da Souza assured Ahruhn that they would be able to assist him in getting settled in his future homeland. His final stop at Durban would be one of necessity – namely, to restock food and provisions for the long journey across the Atlantic. The *Cochin* sailed from Bombay in mid-January and arrived in Port of Spain at the end of May. Ahruhn and Mary, having fulfilled British landing requirements accompanied their two newly acquired friends, who wasted no time in getting to the train station and heading for San Fernando.

Carlos Ferreira and Gaspar da Costa were cousins. They were travelling merchants, who had visited several countries in Africa, the East and more recently, the West Indies. They had relatives with established business in San Fernando, a town which was popular with a number of Portuguese small enterprise businessmen. One of these relatives, Manuel Carvalho, managed a grocery store or 'shop' on the ground floor of his building on Chacon Street. He used the second storey as a guesthouse, offering three rooms for accommodation. It was here, that Ahrun and Mary stayed for a week, during which time they sought modest lodgings to rent. Immediately, Ahruhn went in search of employment as a bookkeeper. Manuel Carvalho advised him to wear western-style clothing since most of the business houses were owned by the English. Ahruhn realised that it might also be an asset for him to learn to speak English fluently as English was the official language of the island.

Within one week of his arrival in Trinidad, Ahruhn had two interviews. The first was with the manager of a sizeable clothing store on High Street. As he entered the establishment, he observed that all the employees were Caucasian and those he heard speaking did so with an English accent. He felt very uncomfortable during his fifteen-minute interview and changed his mind about wanting to work there before he even left the store. He did not return to receive the verdict.

His second encounter was more successful. Mr MacCrae, a Scottish plantation owner, was in the process of setting up a hardware store. He needed a mature, responsible person to perform several tasks, 'a jack of all trades,' because he had a full-time job. Mr MacCrae was delighted to hear that Ahruhn was an experienced bookkeeper and had evidence to prove the fact. Ahruhn wasted no time in proving himself efficient.

Although he assumed both managerial responsibilities and bookkeeping duties, he reserved some time for him and Mary to walk through the streets of the town in search of a plot of land. The majority of proprietors in San Fernando were Europeans – English, Scottish, French and Portuguese. Only a few East Indians owned land in the town and they were not interested in selling. Eventually, he was able to purchase half an acre from a French Creole businessman who wished to move to Port of Spain. Mr MacCrae was instrumental in this venture.

The spot was located on the far south of the town, which was quite some distance from his workplace – a situation that encouraged him to devise a plan. Since they were so close to the Crossroads, where people entering San Fernando from Princes Town sought transportation to the wharf and shopping area, he was positive he would be successful in entering the buggy business. With this plan in mind, Ahruhn and Mary decided to rear a few horses; their love for and knowledge of these animals was all the encouragement they needed. At first, he bought one buggy and employed one driver, Gopaul. Then one evening, while he was helping Gopaul unfasten the carriage from the horse, he was approached by two men. They were Gopaul's friends and were looking for work as buggy drivers. At first, Ahruhn was hesitant to invest his savings and expand his business so soon, but Mary encouraged him to use one of the drivers to ply a new route where a buggy service was needed. Ahruhn took her advice and used Gopaul, who was more familiar with the town than the two newcomers, to work within the residential areas of San Fernando. It was a good decision and Gopaul was able to provide a reliable buggy service to the residents of San Fernando who could afford it.

When he was able to realise a steady income from his new venture, Ahruhn went in search of a second property, one closer to the commercial and administrative centre of the town. Mr MacCrae recommended a lawyer to him, one whom he thought was open-minded. Mr Hobson advised Ahruhn to have his marriage registered and also that his wife's name be included on his legal documents as he had no other relatives in Trinidad, excepting his immediate family.

Ahruhn was contented with his financial situation. He considered himself fortunate to have met Mr MacCrae, whom he thought a very agreeable person and who appreciated Ahruhn's work. Mr MacCrae had a positive attitude towards him and had even assisted Ahruhn by offering advice. However, in this new homeland, life was lonely. Beyond the workplace and behind the closed doors at nightfall, Ahruhn and Mary felt isolated. They yearned for the loving support of family members and the familiarity of a village community that they had left behind. They were both anxious to have a large family, a house full of children to fill the void of an empty dwelling and memories of their native homelands. Within six years they were blessed with four children.

One afternoon, after having completed her

domestic chores, Mary settled into the hammock to take a rest. Her two older children were playing on the floor beside her on the small porch; the two younger ones were asleep in a bedroom and Gopaul was cleaning the buggy. She was roused by an approaching call, '*Salaam, salaam!*' A grey-haired, middle-aged, balding man had entered the yard. He was walking towards the house and held two leather-bound books close to his chest. She stood up and moved slowly towards the front entrance of the house.

The man was wearing western clothing but spoke Hindi. 'My name is Ramesh Chandoo and I am a catechist in the Susamachar Church,' he introduced himself. 'I want to invite you and your family to a special gathering of all our new believers on Sunday at ten o'clock.' He paused briefly, turned sideways to face Gopaul, and then added, 'And you are invited too,' as he traced an arched wave of his right hand to include Gopaul in the invitation. He turned to Mary and bowed.

The visitor was not unexpected. San Fernando was a small town and they lived within walking distance of the new Mission church and school. She was aware of the missionaries' quest to convert her people to Christianity, but she and Ahruhn had never discussed the possibility of changing their religion. They were not very religious, even though they were both Muslim. They would have to discuss this situation, especially as their children would now be involved.

'Thank you for the invitation,' she said in Hindi. 'I cannot promise you that we will come; I have four small children and taking them with me will be very difficult. Maybe, another time will be better when they are older,' she said. 'But I would like to send the children to school,' she added.

'Of course,' he replied. 'But remember, you are always welcome at Church.' He bowed again and walked out of the yard.

Ahruhn was not opposed to his children's attending the Christian school. In Trinidad, the colonial rulers had provided their state religion and education for freed Africans, and the French Creoles had done the same for Roman Catholics; but the indentured Indians were expected to return to their homeland. However, repatriation was being discouraged and India had sunken into the depths of political and economic chaos. There was no turning back. Ahruhn decided that for the time being, his family would attend the Christian church. In any case, Christianity was not unknown to him and his people, the Persians. He remembered his father saying that thousands of years ago the Israelites were allowed safe passage through their lands as they fled from Egypt. Like the Christians, he too believed in one God. Mary had no problem with his decision. The whole family attended church occasionally. The two older children, Alice and Sarah, enrolled at Grant School but Ahruhn and Mary postponed their conversion to a later date.

Mr MacCrae's hardware business exceeded his expectations. Thanks to Ahruhn's untiring dedication and Mr MacCrae's constant scrutiny of Ahruhn's bookkeeping, they were a successful pair. The store became cluttered and untidy because there was simply no space to stock recently imported goods, which were ordered for an increasing number of new customers. Eventually, the decision was made to move to more spacious premises and, with some additional help, Mr MacCrae's 'one-stop' hardware store was transformed into Southern Hardware and Supplies.

One afternoon Alice came home with an envelope addressed to 'Mr and Mrs Ahmed.'

'The teacher sent it, Ma; she said it's from the catechist, Mr Chandoo,' Alice reported. Mary left the envelope unopened for her husband to read. When Ahruhn saw it, he smiled. 'They can't wait to add up the numbers of the new converts,' he commented. He opened the envelope, read the letter silently, then aloud.

'Dear Friends,

You are invited to a Baptism Service every first Sunday of the month at 10 a.m. at the Susamachar Presbyterian Church, when we will witness the conversion of our new church members and welcome them into our congregation. Everyone is invited.
We hope you will attend.

I am,

Yours in Faith,

Ramesh Chandoo.'

After the children went to bed that evening, Ahruhn and Mary discussed the probability of their accepting the invitation. Mary was surprised at her husband's response, when he said, 'You know, Mary, I think as a family we should all join the church.'

'When, now?' she asked.

'The sooner, the better,' he replied. 'Our children will be able to attend school and will be better able to live in this part of the world. Who knows? We may not be returning to India for some time.'

'We may accept a new religion, Ahruhn, but we cannot change ourselves; we are too old for that,' she said.

'We know that, but the church does not understand that. I am really thinking about our children,' he replied. 'What will be their position if they cannot communicate with the people who control their lives? If they remain here, they must not be isolated like our people are right now. They must find a way to improve their position in this society and gain acceptance by all. Right now, Indians are not even considered a part of this society. They provide labour and that is all. Some return to India, but for those who remain, there is nothing. If they don't try to change and adapt to this new way of life, they will always be labourers,' he added.

'You trying to change the world, Ahruhn?' Mary asked her husband.

'No, just trying to improve it,' he said with a faint smile. He paused; he knew this was difficult for his wife. Then he said, 'I will write a letter to Mr Chandoo letting him know we will be at the service next Sunday. At least, we should know what is involved if we decide to join the new religion.' Mary was silent.

Ahruhn took his whole family to church the following Sunday and after the service, had a word with

Mr Chandoo. From a distance, Mary saw the catechist's countenance transform. He smiled. She knew what had transpired. Ahruhn had decided that they should all join the new church. When they climbed into the buggy to go home, Mary said to him, 'Take us for a long ride, Ahruhn. I need some fresh air. I want to catch my breath before I can stand on this soil again.'

On the Sunday afternoon prior to the next baptism service, Mr Chandoo and Reverend James Scott visited the Ahmed family. Ahruhn and Mary were briefed on the details of the baptism ceremony. The Minister explained to them that it was customary for the Church to bestow a Christian name on the convert 'as a symbol of spiritual rebirth to the new faith.' He showed Ahruhn a list of names taken from the Bible and asked him to select one.

'You may keep one or more of your names, if you so desire,' he said. 'I would also like to offer you my name, Scott, as a sign of togetherness and to show that you will always remain one of the precious flock.' He turned to Mary and said, 'You, my child, have been blessed with the holiest of names – that of the mother of Christ.' Ahruhn selected the first name on the list which the Minister gave to him and said he wanted to keep his first name. Reverend James Scott opened his notebook and wrote:

James Scott Aaron

Mary Hari Aaron

Then, he added the children's names:

Alice Aaron

Sarah Aaron

Ariana Aaron

Harvey Aaron.

One Saturday morning, Mr MacCrae informed Ahruhn that he had some business to attend to in Port of Spain. He was planning to leave San Fernando on Sunday and would not be back until Tuesday afternoon. Ahruhn was given the added responsibility of opening the store on Monday morning, securing the money from sales made on that day, ensuring the store entrance was carefully locked before he left on Monday afternoon and re-opening the store on Tuesday morning. Sam, the handyman, would be present to help. Ahruhn was not enthusiastic about his new role; however, he felt the situation was only temporary and hopefully he could learn something from this new experience. He was pleased, nevertheless, that his employer trusted him. The following Monday was very busy. Many peasant farmers were in town and after the day's sales, purchased items had to be replaced on the shelves. On Monday evening, he was exhausted and decided that he would leave home an hour earlier than usual on Tuesday morning to put the store in order, before it was opened to the public at eight o'clock. When he arrived at the store at seven o'clock on Tuesday morning, he quickly unlocked the door, placed the key in his pocket, entered and closed the door, but forgot to lock it from inside the store. He wasted no time in starting the day's work.

Meanwhile, Mr MacCrae kept his business appointment at the scheduled time and returned to San Fernando earlier than expected. On Tuesday morning, he proceeded to the store as usual. At seven-thirty, he inserted the key into the keyhole, only to realise that the door was unlocked. He panicked. Ahruhn would never be so careless, he thought, he would never leave the door open all night. It was possible that an intruder might be inside, or had been inside and had already left. Cautiously, he stepped to the left side of the closed door, bent over his leather bag and searched for his pistol. Then, he opened the door to a slightly ajar position and peered inside to observe if someone was in the retail section of the store. He saw no one, entered the store and tiptoed towards the storeroom at the back, moving closely along the wall. Through the open doorway, he spotted a figure standing on a ladder and reaching up to the highest shelf for an object with some difficulty. He positioned himself carefully, balanced his weight evenly on both feet, aimed at the figure and fired a single shot. Ahruhn fell to the floor with a thud.

Taking no chances, Mr MacCrae moved towards the fallen figure cautiously and leaned over the body. He could not believe his eyes. How could he not have recognised Ahruhn? He stepped back, let the pistol fall from his hand and sat on the floor.

'Mr MacCrae, Sir?' Sam, the handyman called to him, but he heard nothing. A small crowd was gathering at the doorway, as the next-door storeowner,

Mr Jonas made his way through the onlookers.

'Andrew!' he called to Mr MacCrae. 'What has happened here?' he asked in amazement. He received no reply. Half an hour passed before Mr MacCrae regained his presence of mind.

'Fred,' his almost inaudible voice whispered to Mr Jonas, 'help me take Ahruhn to the hospital.'

'We need to inform the police,' Mr Jonas said, then he turned to Sam and told him, 'Sam, go and make a report at the Police Station. Tell the officer in charge that I would like him to come here right away. Mr MacCrae is in no condition to leave.' After the officer arrived and took a statement from Mr MacCrae, Sam and a few onlookers wrapped Ahruhn's limp body in a long coat, then took him to the hospital.

News of the tragic incident spread quickly along High Street. By nine o'clock that morning, several versions of the incident had developed, one of them reaching Gopaul, who was having one of the buggy wheels repaired on St James Street. He thought of the shortest route possible he could take to reach Ahruhn's home. He coaxed the horse into a quick trot up the hill on High Street, proceeded along Coffee Street, then made it break into a gallop along Cipero Street. Mary heard Gopaul strike the animal with the reins to accelerate as the buggy entered the yard. She rushed to the front entrance of the house to learn what the urgency was all about. Before she could utter a word, Gopaul had brought the buggy to a halt and was shouting at the top of his voice, 'Mai! We have to go to the hospital now. Sahib Ahruhn get shoot in de store an' Sahib MacCrae carry him to de hospital. Bring de chil'ren now, Mai. Come quick!'

'Gopaul,' Mary tried to calm him down. 'How you know this?' she asked him.

'Dohn worry about dat, Mai; de whole town know what happen. Sahib dohn have no family excep' you. We have to go now.'

Mary took a change of clothes for the children and their shoes, while Gopaul helped them climb into the buggy. He raced the horse all the way to the hospital.

As they entered the reception lobby, Mary said to Gopaul, 'Wait here, Beta and keep the children.' She walked towards a nurse, who was seated at a desk writing in a book.

'Good Morning, Nurse,' she said. 'I want to ask about my husband, Ahruhn Ali Ahmed; his boss brought him here after somebody shoot him in the store.' The nurse stopped writing and looked up at Mary. She seemed English. 'Wait here,' she said. She stood up, turned around and proceeded to walk towards a curtained area where patients were admitted. A white man, who was seated on a chair in the corner, approached the nurse and spoke to her. Then he looked in Mary's direction and walked towards her. He extended his right hand but she did not respond.

'I am Mr MacCrae,' he said. 'You are Ahruhn's wife?' he asked.

'Oh yes, Sahib. I am Mary; I met you once at your store,' she recalled. 'What happen to Ahruhn?' she asked.

He was silent for a few seconds, lowered his head, looked at her and said, 'Your husband has had a terrible accident; he's been shot accidentally. I thought he was an intruder because it was so early in the morning. I did not expect him to be at work so early. I'm so sorry, Mrs Ahmed.'

'Is he alive?' she asked him.

'Yes, but he is very weak. The doctor said he lost a great deal of blood,' he replied.

'I want to see him; I want to talk to him,' she pleaded.

'They will not let anyone see him; he has lost consciousness. He is not speaking right now. They say he must rest. We just have to wait and pray for good news,' he added, in an attempt to console her.

The nurse returned to her desk and continued to write in her notebook. A doctor, wearing a white coat, emerged from the curtained room. He walked towards Mr MacCrae and said, 'I'm sorry, Sir; he's gone. We couldn't do much for him. The bullet ruptured his kidney and spleen; he lost a great deal of blood and went into heart failure.' He shook Mr MacCrae's hand, turned around and proceeded towards the curtained room.

Mary covered her mouth with both hands to stifle her screams. Mr MacCrae ran to the corner and grabbed the chair, brought it towards her and helped her to sit. Uncontrollably, tears ran down her face. She kept wiping them away with her *ohrni*, but they kept flowing. Gopaul and the two children came forward. He asked Mr MacCrae, 'What happen, Sahib? What happen to Sahib Ahruhn?'

'He didn't make it,' Mr MacCrae said. 'He died a while ago.'

They were all silent for a few minutes in the effort to grasp the enormity of the situation. No one seemed to know what to do or say next. Mr MacCrae recovered from the shocking news first.

'Wait here,' he said to Gopaul. 'I'll be back shortly.'

He walked towards the nurse and spoke to her. She stood up and entered the curtained room, then returned, accompanied by the doctor. He handed Mr MacCrae a sheet of paper and mentioned 'Death Certificate.'

'The body has to be taken to the mortuary and will be released tomorrow,' he said. Mary came forward.

'Please, Doctor, I want to see my husband,' she pleaded.

For the first time he was aware of her presence. 'Yes, you may, but very briefly,' was his response.

Mr MacCrae walked with her to the curtained room, led her to Ahruhn's bedside and stepped back a few paces to allow her some privacy. A second nurse lifted the white sheet off his face. His expression was one of composure as though he had fallen into a peaceful slumber. She observed that there were no bruises or marks on his face. She reached out to him, holding his shoulders beneath the white cloth then ran her hands along his arms. The nurse drew her away from the bed.

'I want to hold his hands,' she said softly as tears blinded her. Mr MacCrae came to her rescue. He led her out of the room to meet Gopaul and the children.

'I think you should take them home,' he said to Gopaul. 'She has had enough to deal with for the day. I will make arrangements for the funeral and will come by the house later. Will you be staying with her?' he asked.

'Yes, Sahib,' he said. 'I go stay with dem.'

Ahruhn was given a Christian funeral service; Reverend James Scott officiated. The Susamachar Church choir and a small congregation were in attendance. The staff and students of Grant School were represented. Following the church service, the cortege proceeded to Paradise Cemetery, where Ahruhn was laid to rest.

Mary kept the two older children at home for one week as she was simply unable to cope with the daily routine of life. During that time, Gopaul proved himself a dependable friend and helper in domestic affairs and in managing the buggy business. When he was not busy, he took the children for buggy rides and cooked the evening meal. The children could not believe that Papa had not come home. Mary encouraged them into thinking that he had gone away on a long trip – probably to India and would rejoin them at a much later date. She felt guilty about this and vowed to reveal the whole truth, when they reached an age of understanding.

When a week of mourning had passed, Mary paid Ahruhn's lawyer a visit. Her assets included a small bank account, two properties and the buggy business. She realised she would have to devise a way of earning an income and thought of opening a shop. She sought Mr Carvalho's advice and visited him on Chacon Street. He recommended certain merchants to her and gave her very important guidelines concerning managing business finances. Thanks to her departed husband, she had learnt some basics from their 'after-dinner' conversations. She had observed how he kept Mr MacCrae's accounts in a large notebook that he often brought home to complete his day's work. She decided that three buggies were too many for her to manage and sold two of them to the drivers whom Ahruhn had employed; the third she kept for her own use. Having discussed her plans with Gopaul and persuaded him to remain in her employ, Mary Hari's Shop and Provisions was opened and one year later, expanded into the Junction Shop and Refreshment Parlour.

When her eldest daughter Alice was fourteen, Mary Hari had two wooden houses constructed on the Gordon Street property, one of which she rented to a young promising local lawyer and the second became her new family home. The children all attended Grant School and were staunch members of the Susamachar Sunday School and the Susamachar congregation. The girls excelled in the current subjects of the day. Alice enjoyed practising her acquired skills by cooking for the family; Sarah developed her talent of drawing and painting; and Ariana's love for baking and dressmaking later proved to be very rewarding as her family grew larger. Harvey followed in his father's footsteps. In San Fernando, Ariana and her family lived among the fortunate few. They enjoyed a privilege, which only a very small minority of East Indians had. They lived in a town, a luxury usually reserved for the upper class of West Indian society in the early twentieth century. East Indians were not entitled to freedom of movement. Indentured labourers were confined to their assigned plantations, while workers with expired contracts were obliged to identify themselves by showing their Certificates of Exemption to officers of the law when they visited the town.

San Fernando was a municipality, a self-governing entity. Its residents boasted of a thriving seaport, shopping facilities, a postal service, a local newspaper, a cinema and horseracing track. Churches and schools were built for Christian believers of three denominations. The focal attraction of the town was its promenade, which reminded one of the English Avenue. Harris Promenade, named after an English governor, consisted of a wide, spacious boulevard where the town proudly displayed its religious, administrative and judicial buildings – a courthouse, town hall, police station and churches were prominent buildings. At one end of the promenade was the San Fernando Colonial Hospital and at the other end was the Carnegie Free Library. Tall flamboyant trees provided shade to benches beneath them and mothers took their young children to play and relax there on afternoons. Ariana and her sister, Alice, were among them; and sometimes on Saturday afternoons, fathers also accompanied their families. Ariana's husband, Clarence, was often one of them.

Clarence Stephen Sanowar was an unusual blend of the influences of Eastern and Western cultures. Hardworking and deeply committed to his profession, he displayed a simple, modest nature. At school, he was entrusted with the task of guiding and motivating the teachers on his staff, in both their academic and religious instruction. He shared camaraderie with them, prolonging his working day, whenever he was requested to help solve any problems they encountered. With his students, he was a strict disciplinarian and showed little patience for failure and laziness. He used a leather strap to discipline older students, who were late for school and careless in their work. Excellence was his school's motto.

On weekdays, Mr Sanowar's routine began at five-thirty in the morning. He knelt at his bedside to praise the Almighty and thank Him for all His bounties; then he proceeded to his backyard to feed and water his animals. He prepared his own breakfast – a simple meal of bread, butter, cheese and a hot cocoa beverage. Dressed in trousers, long-sleeved shirt, jacket and tie, at seven o'clock he was ready and waiting in front of his house to board the buggy which took him to Vistabella Presbyterian School. On afternoons, he walked home.

Saturday mornings were devoted to Bible instruction for teachers, who were also Sunday school teachers. On Sundays, the school was used as a place of worship for adults, as well as for the children's Sunday school classes. On Saturday, when he left school at midday, Mr Sanowar met Manwar, his brother, at the San Fernando market, where he usually interacted with some of his East Indian friends and had an opportunity to speak in his native tongue. Sunday was a special family day. Every member of the family attended either Sunday school or the adult service at the Susamachar Church in San Fernando and the rest of the day was spent at home.

Mr Sanowar's work at school progressed

continuously, but in Trinidad, difficult economic times brought his family financial hardship. Sugar had long declined as the major export produce, and cocoa markets abroad had shrunken because of wartime activities. Firstly, there was the Spanish–American War, then the First World War. There were food shortages and as a result, food prices soared. Cutting costs was not an option; it was a necessity. Mr Sanowar built a second fowl coop to keep more chickens and got two goats from Manwar. Myrtle, the helper, baked bread twice weekly in the brick oven and the children were encouraged to make use of the fruit and coconuts from the backyard, and to cease making candies and pies. At the end of the month, Mr Sanowar bought one bag of rice, one bag of flour and one bag of sugar. He did not have to purchase cocoa sticks and vegetables, which Manwar supplied weekly. Occasionally, usually at Easter or Christmas, he would kill a goat and invite Alice and her family, Indrani and Manwar.

In spite of these difficulties, Mr Sanowar continued to observe his children's performance at school. He encouraged them to be constantly diligent in two aspects of life, their schoolwork and their devotion to the Almighty. Intuitively, he knew that his two elder daughters, Lily and Cynthia, would be successful teachers; it was unfortunate that there was no secondary school for them to attend. His two elder sons, James and Ben were lucky in that respect. He expressed his concerns to his wife, Ariana – fondly addressed as Anna – about the children's drawbacks. James was asthmatic and was obliged to remain at home on some schooldays; Ben was very playful and even truant occasionally. His third son, Waldo, was only nine, but showed a keen interest in the plants and animals whenever they were together in the backyard.

One night after the children had gone to bed, and Ariana was tidying the living room, a fight broke out in the boys' room. Mr Sanowar's first impulse was to give all three of them a solid thrashing, but Ariana restrained him. 'Don't beat them, Clarence. Find out what the problem is first,' she advised.

When he entered the room, he couldn't believe what he saw. Ben was pretending to be sleeping on the mattress, which lay on the floor. James and Waldo had covered themselves with the sheet, exposing the wooden base of the bed all around them.

'What's the problem here?' he asked angrily. James spoke first. He uncovered his head and turned to face his father.

'We can't fit on the bed, Pa,' he uttered in a pleading tone.

'Nonsense!' shouted Mr Sanowar.

'De mattress keep falling off de bed, Pa,' Ben joined in the conversation as he quickly changed into a sitting position and leaned against the partition.

'Speak to me properly, boy!' Mr Sanowar shouted at him. 'Where did you learn that gibberish?' He stepped forward and grabbed Ben's full head of hair.

'Sorry, Pa,' Ben apologised.

'Ben,' he ordered, 'put back the mattress on the bed and tidy the sheet. Go to bed now and behave yourselves. I don't want to hear a sound from you until tomorrow morning.' He was about to leave the room, but turned around and asked, 'Did you boys say your prayers tonight?'

'No, Pa,' all three chorused.

'Well!' he paused for them to start moving. 'Get down on your knees and ask the merciful Father to guide you in your thoughts and actions – especially you, Ben.'

When he closed the door behind him and entered the living room, he said to Ariana, 'Ann, we have to get another bed made for them, one for Ben to sleep on by himself.' Ariana said nothing, but she was well aware of the children's situation. They were growing up quickly and needed more than one extra bed. They all needed more space and a larger house. The big problem was money and that, they did not have.

In a week's time, Mr Sanowar located a carpenter on the northern outskirts of the town, not far from his school in Vistabella. Mr Payne, a Barbadian, built Ben's bed on a Saturday afternoon. Ben had to do his part as well. He husked the coconuts, stripped and cleaned the coconut fibre, and filled the sack that Ariana had sewn from bleached flour bags. Then she made a second casing from store-bought material to protect Ben from the coconut fibre's uncomfortable roughness.

Ariana paid her mother a visit to discuss her family's problem and to seek Mary Hari's advice. She took Annette, Ben and Waldo with her. As they approached Mary Hari's house, she was surprised to see Gopaul offloading some small items of furniture and boxes containing kitchen utensils. Her mother, who was standing at the bottom of the stairs, was instructing him where to place the items.

'What's going on, Gopaul, you moving in down-stairs?' she asked, smiling.

'No, no, Beti!' he exclaimed. 'Ah jus' helping yuh Mai bring a few t'ings home.'

Mary Hari walked closer towards them and spoke to Ariana, 'I so sorry about that, Beti. I forget to tell you that I decided to close the business at the Crossroads. I think it served its purpose and to be honest,' she placed her two hands on her large hips, 'I am tired. And you know, Gopaul opened his own rum shop in Princes Town, so when we ready for a drink we know where to go!'

Gopaul laughed. She stepped out into the street and looked in the wagon to see if there were any more boxes to be offloaded and asked Ariana, 'You and the children taking a walk?'

'No, Ma,' Ariana answered. 'I came to see you. I want to discuss something with you – about the house.'

'Come, Beti; let's go upstairs. This sounds serious.'

The children were following them up the stairs and Ariana said to the boys, 'Ben, you and Waldo stay and help Gopaul. Annette, come with me.'

When they were seated, Ariana's mother asked her, 'what's wrong, child? You look so worried.'

'Ma, we need more space in the house for the children and I was thinking if we could get the house extended, we could add on two bedrooms for them. You know, Ma, just now James will be going to the Boys' College and Lily and Cynthia are thinking of attending Teachers' College. These children are growing up fast.

Three big girls cannot share one room; in the next year or two, they will need a little privacy. Right now, they all sit at the dining room table to study and do their homework. The other children are always disturbing them and I'm sure that is very bad.' Ariana finished, feeling slightly relieved after sharing her grievances with her mother.

'So, what your husband think about all of this?' Mary Hari asked.

'Ma, Clarence doesn't know I am here; he hasn't even thought of this problem. Well, he hasn't said anything to me about it. He had a bed made for Ben last week because the three boys couldn't fit on one bed, but he knows that very soon we have to do something to change the situation. The big problem is he cannot do much.' Ariana's voice began to break as emotion stifled her words. 'You think you could help us get a loan from the bank, Ma?' she asked.

'A loan, my child?' her mother asked in disbelief. 'To mortgage your property! Who is going to pay back that loan? You think Clarence can afford that, with all these children both of you have? Oh no, Beti, you cannot do that! You could lose your house like that, or die before you finish paying for it.

'So what you think we could do, Ma?' Ariana asked.

'You know what I think; I think you must talk to Clarence first. If you really serious about extending the house, he will have to borrow some money – not from the bank, but from a good friend or family and still make a legal paper for protection. I will ask around to find out which builder can do a good job without overcharging you. Don't worry too much. This will take a little time, Beti; you have to be patient about this one,' Mary Hari said to her. 'In the meantime, discuss the situation with your husband,' she advised Ariana.

Ariana felt she had broached a problem over which she had no control. As the days went by, she thought of ways to break the subject to Clarence. She knew he had a great deal of responsibility at school and had other issues on his mind. He was an honest and caring person, but was inclined to keep his problems to himself. She was not sure why he behaved this way. It might have resulted from his difficult circumstances as a young man. He was expected to solve the family's problems as he was the older male member of the family after his father had died. Or, it could simply be the natural behaviour of the male ego.

The school year was at the end of its first term; by the end of the third term, three of their four eldest children would be writing examinations to enter educational institutions at a higher level. She wanted them to be successful, but did not know how she could contribute to their success and wondered how and when this situation would be rectified.

As the examination dates grew closer Mr Sanowar became more concerned about his children's academic progress. After school, Lily, James, Cynthia and Rose became his personal pupils. He checked their exercise books to monitor their day's work and helped them improve in their weak areas. He extended the time spent at school for two reasons. At home, he was sure the younger children were noisy on afternoons; also, he could reduce the amount of kerosene oil used in the lamps, if the children did less schoolwork at home during the night. Three of his 'after school' scholars wrote and passed the Post Primary examination with commendable scores. James wrote the entrance examination to Naparima College, a Secondary boys' school founded by the Canadians. Rose expressed her ambition to become a nurse and pursued the current nurses' training programme at the San Fernando Colonial Hospital. Lily and Cynthia entered the Naparima Teachers' Training College in Paradise Pasture in San Fernando, an institution established by Canadian educators to produce the calibre of teachers that was needed in their schools. The one-year programme was comprehensive and catered for both the spiritual and academic needs of young students. Teachers-in-training studied several subjects: English Grammar, Arithmetic, Algebra, Bible Study, The Life of Christ, History and Geography. In Trinidad, more Primary schools were being built and more teachers were needed.

Mr Sanowar was proud of his two elder daughters and anticipated their joining his teachers at Vistabella, when they completed their course of study. The number of students at his school had increased to two hundred and he needed more trained teachers. When the ladies had graduated, both joined him at Vistabella; but one year later, Cynthia was transferred to Naparima Girls' High School, the first Protestant Secondary school for girls in South Trinidad. There, Cynthia quickly became involved in the association, Trinidad Girls in Training. This body organised extra curricular group activities, designed to nurture Christian values among young women and simultaneously assist them in becoming mature, well-rounded individuals in society. The groups went camping, held retreats and assisted in organising fund-raising activities beneficial to the Presbyterian schools and churches. The principal had commented to Mr Sanowar that his daughter was particularly successful in working with junior students at the school, and recommended that she participate in a series of education courses scheduled to be held at the San Fernando Government Anglican Elementary School on Harris Promenade. These were organised by the Department of Education.

At the beginning of James' second year at Naparima College, Harvey, Ariana's brother, left San Fernando to work at an accounting firm in Port of Spain. Mary Hari told Ariana that James was welcome to stay with her. He would have his own room, and all the peace and quiet he needed to study his schoolwork. Ariana was pleased with her mother's offer, but James had mixed feelings. Mr Sanowar also seemed pleased and thanked Mary Hari but Ariana knew he wanted his son to be at home with them so that he could share some of James' experiences at secondary school, an educational institution, which he himself had not been fortunate enough to attend.

It was the middle of a two-week Easter vacation for all schoolchildren. Ariana was creaming butter and sugar to make an Easter cake. The family's teachers were at school preparing for special Easter presentations. James was at his school library; Ben, Waldo and Annette were picking mangoes and Rose was helping Ariana. There was a gentle knock on the side entrance of the dining room. When Ariana opened the door, Alice and her daughter, Ida, appeared, each holding a bottle wrapped in brown paper.

'Just in time for you to put in the cake, Sis,' she said, lifting the bottle of rum out of the brown paper bag and placing it on the dining room table. Ida rested her bottle on the table, stepped towards Ariana and kissed her, then walked towards Rose and whispered something to her. The two girls left the room and went to meet the younger children in the backyard.

'You know I can't use that in this house; but thanks anyway. Maybe for Christmas, I'll make you a fruit cake,' Ariana suggested.

'Well, we have so much at home I had to bring you two bottles,' her sister answered.

'What's happening at your house?' Ariana couldn't imagine what her sister was trying to say.

'Well,' she started to explain, 'last night Harold came home drunk, complaining that one of his customers gave him a big disappointment. He had placed an order for materials to build a house and then was not able to sell enough sugar cane and cocoa to pay for it. So, he cancelled the order.'

'I'm sure another customer will need the materials,' Ariana assured her.

'Unfortunately, it seems that business is not very good these days. Harold said the sawmill is not making money; he can get trees to cut and people to work, but nobody is buying. The big ships are at war; only guns are selling these days and we are at their mercy. Ration cards will soon be out again and people will scarcely have any money for food. Believe it or not, the two thriving businesses now depend on oil for the rich and rum for the poor,' Alice concluded.

'So maybe Harold will venture into the rum shop business?' Ariana speculated.

'Who knows? Anything can happen these days,' was the reply.

Alice and Ida left to visit their seamstress to collect their Easter dresses. The family was invited to a special Easter function for businessmen over the coming weekend. Harold Ramrattan was a successful sawmill owner from Princes Town, but his family lived on lower Gordon Street. He was originally Hindu and was baptised into the Presbyterian religion before he married Alice. He had one daughter and two sons, who were fairly close in age to Ariana's older children. In comparison with her family, Alice's was wealthy. They lived in a two-storey house, owned a carriage and two horses, and often entertained their friends at home. Her house was always clean and well kept as she could afford to have two helpers for the household chores. Alice's lifestyle made it obvious that her family had money to spend. Sometimes, Ariana was envious of her sister's material acquisitions and wondered if her own financial situation would ever improve.

Ariana was waiting on Myrtle to open the brick oven, when she heard a horse and wagon stop in the street. She recognised Clarence's voice. He must have been to the wholesale shop to buy foodstuff for the month. She entered the dining room and looked through the jalousies. The wagon driver had unloaded three large sacks, most likely containing flour, sugar and rice. The two men lifted the sacks and leaned them against the outer wall of the dining room, after which the driver left. She walked towards the entrance to the dining room and asked him, 'Are you ready for lunch?'

'In a minute,' he answered. He bent over the tap near the washtub, turned it open, washed his hands and dried them with a small towel, hanging overhead on the clothesline. He then entered the dining room and sat on his chair, at the head of the table. The children had already eaten, but Ariana had waited for him so that they could have lunch together. She observed that he was slightly agitated. He sipped a little water from his glass, pulled his chair closer to the table, for a second time, and cleared his throat. 'You feeling all right, Clarence?' she asked him.

'You have to see what I saw this morning,' he said. She was surprised at the suddenness of his remark and was unsure how she should respond.

'Something good or bad?' she asked.

'I'm not saying – wait until you see for yourself,' he said, keeping her in suspense.

'It's not like you to play games, Clarence. It can't be something bad. You have a plan?' she asked, becoming curious about his intentions. A smile came over his face. He clasped his hands, bowed his head and uttered prayerfully, 'Dear Father in Heaven, for these and all Thy mercies, we thank Thee.'

Ariana waited for her two elder daughters to return home before accompanying her husband on his mysterious visit. She put Annette to bed after lunch, but Clarence said that Ben and Waldo would go with them. The household needed a break from their noise and unending activity. The first leg of their mission was walking to the location where the mystery lurked.

They proceeded from the south of Gordon Street, along Court Street, across Harris Promenade, down High Street and finally to the Wharf. Before them stood a grey and weather-beaten wooden, two-storey building. Its broken shutters, damaged roofing and cracked, peeling paint provoked a negative reaction from Ariana. At the front and sides of the building several tall crate-like wooden structures stood, as if waiting for something to happen. The rear of the building was not visible to them. Ariana was confused. 'What is this about, Clarence?' she asked.

'I came here this morning,' he explained, 'and there were about twenty workmen, hammering away in their noisy activity. Most of them were engaged in building those wooden platforms you see there.' He pointed to the tall crates at which she was looking. She thought they might be used for transportation of a certain commodity, since they were in a busy commercial area. He continued, 'The workmen have gone home now, but this morning I recognised three men who had worked on my new school. When I asked them what they were building, they said they were using huge jacks to raise the building onto those platforms that they have already built. They would then replace the platforms with greenheart posts. This area floods when the tide is high. They will repair the building to be used as the new Southern Railway Headquarters. The construction company that is working here is the same one that built my school and other Presbyterian schools. It is owned by Canadians. Anna, I am going to ask Reverend Scott to introduce me to the foreman, so he could help us with our house,' he concluded.

'And the money?' she asked wide-eyed and still puzzled.

'I think Manwar will be able to help us with that; he is a rich man now, you know. He owns three long wagons and delivers cane to the St Madeline factory,' he answered.

'And when we going to do this, Clarence?' she asked him again.

'After the Easter weekend, I will go to see the Minister. If the foreman agrees to work during the August vacation, when the children will be on holiday, that will be great! Anna, I need your help and support on this one. Say a prayer, Anna. Say a prayer for us and the children. We need this. We need James and the girls to stay with us as long as they want to – until they are ready to have their own families.' He was filled with emotion. Ariana had never seen her husband so moved, except, of course, when a newborn was added to the family. Clarence held her hands gently, guiding her movement as she turned around. They paused for a while then started to retrace their steps homewards. His call to Ben and Waldo broke the spell that was cast over her. 'For now Anna,' he said to her, 'for now, let this be our secret. When I talk to the Minister and Manwar, then we will know for sure what is happening. If the plan works out, we will tell Mai and every body else – but not before then.'

Reverend James Scott did not forget Mr Sanowar's request. A company supervisor, Mr Archibald, arrived at the Sanwar residence at ten o'clock on the Saturday morning before school re-opened for the second term that year. He was pleasant and businesslike. He said he wanted to discuss the extent of the work requested, the conditions required during the working period and the estimated cost of the project. Mr Sanowar explained that he needed more space for his family and would like to have a ground floor with floorboards. Mr Archibald suggested brick walls as a strong support to the upper floor and hollow cylindrical iron posts to strengthen the overhanging front gallery.

'We will supply all the materials – with exception of wood – as well as labour,' he informed Mr Sanowar. You will be responsible for getting the floorboards and any windows or doors you may need. The actual raising of the house will take one week and the rest of the work, another week; so let's say two weeks. However, you will have to vacate the premises for that period of time. If we have to take more time, it will be at our cost,' he added with a wry smile. They walked around the house and stopped at the back. 'You will need a covered staircase here,' he pointed out. He took out a pencil and small notebook from his shirt pocket and started to write. Mr Sanowar invited him to come inside and sit at the dining room table to make his notes. A few minutes later, the gentleman stood up and announced, 'Sir, it will cost you eighty pounds. When do you want us to begin?' he asked.

'The second week in August,' replied Mr Sanowar. 'Will that be convenient for you?' he asked.

'Oh, yes. Well, I'll be off now. If you need to contact me, you can do so through the Reverend. Good morning to you, Sir.'

'Thank you, thank you for coming,' said Mr Sanowar. They shook hands and he watched his visitor make a brisk exit.

Ariana couldn't wait to tell her mother and Alice the good news. Alice's husband, Harold, offered to sell Mr Sanwar all the floorboards he needed at cost price.

'Is a real shame,' he said to him. 'But ah jus' cyah make money off yuh, Clarence; after all yuh is meh family. Remember, yuh have to get transportation.'

'I'm grateful for all the help you can give, Harold,' replied Mr Sanowar. 'Manwar will provide transportation. He will collect the boards and deliver them to my house in his long wagon.'

Ariana's mother was also taking advantage of Harold's offer to sell wood at cost price. She told Ariana, 'I'm building another small house on my land, and the rent will go towards paying for the boards you are buying from Harold. I want to make a contribution.'

'Oh Ma, you didn't have to do that,' Ariana moaned.

'And if I don't help my daughter, who will?' she asked.

Before the summer vacation commenced, Ariana began to store her ornaments and wall hangings in boxes. She felt helpless that she was unable to make a monetary contribution towards the renovation of the house and compensated for this by keeping herself fully occupied. She thought her three working daughters should play a part in their father's repayment of the debt incurred, and suggested that they should each contribute two dollars monthly.

For the two-week period during which time the house had to be vacated, the family was separated. Ariana accepted Alice's offer to spend some time at the Los Iros beach; she took Ben, Waldo and Annette with her. The working ladies decided to attend a TGIT retreat and camp at Mayaro, which was usually planned by Cynthia's school during the month of August. Mr Sanowar and James stayed with Mary Hari.

Work progressed on the house as scheduled. Mr Archibald introduced Mr Sanowar to his foreman, who arrived with his workers promptly at seven o'clock every morning, except on Sunday, and left at five o'clock every afternoon. Every morning, Mr Sanowar witnessed their arrival and every evening, their departure. Within the first week of the construction team's work, the house was standing on eight ten-foot-high wooden platforms and work had already started on the brick foundation. In the second week, the first storey brick walls, the windows and doors, and the covered staircase to the back of the house were completed. When the project was almost finished, the foreman said to Mr Sanowar, 'Sir, you will need bathroom facilities upstairs. We can enclose the six-foot-square space adjacent to the landing at the top of the stairs, and also put a banister on either side of the staircase.'

Mr Sanowar had not thought of the bathroom facilities. It would be ridiculous for Ariana to be running down twenty-two steps every time she needed to use the bathroom. He tried to calculate how much a cesspit tank and plumbing for upstairs would cost – and surrendered in the effort.

With Gopaul's assistance, Mary Hari arranged to have the house cleaned and ready for the Sanowar family to resume occupancy of their premises. She and Mr Sanowar were standing below the staircase, admiring the excellent work the construction crew had done. 'I have to congratulate you, Clarence,' she said to him. 'You know, you really have courage and determination. However, I must advise you about one thing – you have to make out a schedule for when you want to go upstairs. You can't be running up and down those steps all the time. They will kill you,' she concluded with a chuckle.

Mr Sanowar and James were the first family members to return to their newly renovated house. Lily, Cynthia and Rose were delighted to see their bedroom elevated to a higher level, where the air was cool and bracing. The younger children scampered through the vacant ground floor area. The family settled into their habitual sleeping places on the first night after their return. On the following day, the furniture and breakable house ware, stored at Alice's home were transported to their rightful place of residence. Mr Sanowar, James and Myrtle followed Ariana's instructions for arranging the furniture. The number of rooms which had existed in the original house was doubled. Mr Sanowar reserved the small front bedroom for James; the former living room and front veranda were his and Ariana's domain. Lily had her own bedroom, that is, until Annette insisted she wanted to sleep with Lily, and Cynthia and Rose occupied the former dining room. Ben and Waldo were cautioned to remain downstairs until they were ready to retire to bed.

When the house was finally reorganised, and the first meal was served, Mr Sanowar engaged all members of his family, as well as Myrtle, their devoted helper, in a thanksgiving service. Subsequently, it became a custom that every evening after dinner the whole family would give thanks to the Father in Heaven for the great gifts he had bestowed on them through their friends, family and well-wishers.

Harvey, Ariana's brother, returned to San Fernando and announced to his mother that he had purchased a lot of land in San Fernando and was thinking of building a house. Mary Hari suspected he was thinking of starting his own family. Prolonged bachelorhood seemed to be making him restless. She herself was not as active as before. She had been to see a doctor at the hospital and was advised that she needed to rest; her blood pressure was high. Rose reported to Ariana that the doctor told Ma to stop driving the buggy and particularly, to stop riding the horse.

'Sell the horses, Ma,' Ariana said to her.

'And pay a cabby driver every time I want to make my shopping?' she retorted.

'No, Ma, just tell Alice when you need a ride. You are getting too old to manage the horse and buggy. You know sometimes these large animals can be difficult,' she cautioned.

'Alice has her own business to deal with – and besides Harvey can use the buggy, now that he is back home,' she responded.

'All right, Ma,' Ariana gave in. 'But, at least, you should stop riding the horse,' she insisted.

When Harvey woke up one morning the following

week, he saw his mother seated in the buggy and holding the horse's reins in her hands, as though transfixed and unable to move. 'Ma!' he shouted. 'You need help – what's wrong?' She did not reply. He ran down the steps, across the yard, stepped into the buggy and held her right hand. She was motionless and said nothing. He lifted her out of the driver's seat, placed her in the passenger seat and took her to the emergency room at the hospital. The doctor admitted her to a ward.

'She has had a mild stroke,' he said to Harvey. 'Fortunately, she did not fall out of the buggy; she could have broken her hip or leg and that would have been a further complication.'

'How long will she be here?' Harvey asked.

'We'll keep her for two days and monitor her progress,' the doctor replied.

In the afternoon, Ariana and Clarence visited her. 'What you doing here, Ma?' Ariana asked her mother.

'I don't know; I don't remember exactly what happened,' she answered. 'I thought I was on High Street making my shopping.'

'You see, Ma, you're lucky that Harvey was still at home and you were not alone. I am living on the same street as you and I might not even realise that you need help. You know, Ma, you need someone to stay with you when Harvey is at work. You don't worry; Alice and I will take care of that,' Ariana assured her mother.

Ariana held her mother's hands and kissed them. 'Oh, Ma,' she said. 'You have to understand that you need to change your routine; you must slow down before it is too late.'

Mary Hari did not survive a second stroke. Her condition deteriorated and the doctor prolonged her stay at the hospital. Three days after she was admitted to hospital she died. When Ariana entered her mother's bedroom to select a burial outfit for her, she observed a sheet of paper on the dressing table. Her name was written on it and it was folded in two. She held it open, observed it had been dated one week previously, and briefly read its contents. It was her mother's will. She quickly folded it, put it in her bag, sat on the bed for a while, and then returned to her task.

Mary Hari was laid to rest at Paradise Cemetery in the same spot as her husband, thirty-five years after his death. Following the funeral service and burial, the entire family met and consoled each other at Alice's residence until late in the evening. Later that week, all of Mary Hari's children were sent copies of her final will by her attorney. She had left a portion of her wealth for each of her children. Her property on Gordon Street she bequeathed to her last daughter. Mr Sanowar couldn't believe Ariana's good fortune.

'So you are a lady of means now – you are a proprietress,' he congratulated her.

'And have been for some time since we owned this piece of land,' she reminded him. 'Now I can help you to complete the work on the house and make it more comfortable,' she added.

'You are a good woman, Anna,' he said.' I couldn't hope to find a better wife.'

Soon Ariana became more reluctant to descend

and climb the long flight of stairs. She complained of tiredness and headaches until Rose asked a doctor from the hospital to visit her.

After he examined her, he announced, 'You're pregnant! Didn't you suspect that?' That possibility had not occurred to Ariana.

'There is a small problem though – you need to rest. You can walk a little; but, every day you must lie down for at least an hour or two,' he advised. 'And this is baby number eight?' he asked.

She smiled.

'Well, Mrs Sanowar, I think your husband should leave well enough alone and find himself another bedroom in the house. You already have a large family,' he added.

Ariana decided she wanted no more children after she gave birth to this child. Mr Sanowar took the doctor's advice, and slept downstairs with Ben and Waldo.

The quiet little town of San Fernando was gradually experiencing a transformation. The oil refinery had been transferred from Point Fortin to Pointe-a-Pierre and this was having an impact on the town. Coal was being replaced by kerosene, a by-product of petroleum. Two- and three-burner stoves ousted the coal pot. Several new stores were opened on High Street, many of which were owned by that first generation of Trinidadians who were children of immigrant families. Ariana acquired two new pastimes, window-shopping and cinema going. Sometimes, Cynthia and Rose accompanied her, but Lily and her husband were never interested. 'A waste of money for a world of make-believe,' Mr Sanowar would say. She ignored his comments and went anyway. It was common knowledge that several commercial houses in Port of Spain and the oil refinery were already using telephones. It was just a matter of time before this facility would be extended to residents. She couldn't wait for her world to change – to expand a little. It had to, otherwise she would explode.

CHAPTER 4

Ties That Bind

Blessed be the ties that bind us
To loved ones in our care.
Blessed be the friends who help
    us
In times of need and fear.
Blessed be the faith that guides
    us,
That Heavenly Light Above
To strengthen and console us,
An assurance of His love.
Blessed be my home away from
    home
Our love that's here to stay
A life to live without regret
A legacy to redirect
Our claim to have and hold.

'Pa, are we going to school this morning?' I called, peeping through the crack in the door to see if he was still in bed. It's past six-thirty.'

'No, Lily,' Ma answered. 'Open the door and come in.'

'Where is Pa? Is something wrong?' I asked her.

'He went to the doctor's office to ask him to come

to see me. I think this baby has a problem – somehow I cannot turn to get off the bed,' Ma explained.

'Did you have breakfast? Can I get you something?' I offered.

'No, Lily, Pa made a cup of tea for me. That's enough for now. Has Myrtle come yet?' she asked. 'I don't think the kitchen is open.'

'Don't worry, Ma; I'll go downstairs to see,' I answered.

It was Pa's habit to open the kitchen early and make breakfast for Ma, himself and me, every morning before we left for school. I was teaching at Pa's school – having passed my teaching examination – and we left for school early, leaving my younger siblings to follow later on.

Myrtle was our hardworking and devoted helper, who lived one street away and arrived at seven o'clock promptly every morning, except on Sunday. As I was lifting the latch of the kitchen door, Myrtle appeared.

'Good morning, Miss Lily. Leh me help yuh wit' dat. Pa oversleep dis morning?' she queried.

'Worse than that, Myrtle, Ma sick and can't come off the bed – so Pa went to get the doctor,' I explained.

'Oh meh sweet Jesus, help yuh poor Ma! – too many children, meh chile. So she dohn move off de bed for de whole night?' Myrtle asked.

'I don't think so – but I'm not sure,' I hesitated.

'Miss Lily, bring up de bedpan for she now. Mrs Sanowar mus' be dying to go to de bathroom,' she said. Myrtle hardly ever went to Ma's room, so I took the bedpan upstairs and helped Ma.

When Pa returned from the doctor's office, he said

the doctor would arrive about nine o'clock, so he would remain at home until then. I agreed to take Pa's Bible classes at school that day and Pa said he would ask Deo, the buggy driver, to take us home as soon as school was dismissed in the afternoon – in case Ma's condition deteriorated.

When I saw Pa later that day at school, he said that the doctor told Ma to stay in bed for the whole morning. He gave her an injection and took a urine sample.

'Why was that necessary?' I asked Pa.

'Dr Kroeh said Ma might have sugar in her urine – diabetes.'

'Is that bad, Pa?' I got worried.

'I really don't know – it depends on what Dr Kroeh finds in the urine,' he said.

'Pa, is the baby causing Ma to be sick?' I asked.

'Why do you think so?' he asked, looking puzzled.

'Because Myrtle said Ma had too many children – it's time for her to stop having any more.' I could see he was not impressed by Myrtle's comment.

Ma was sick for almost the whole of that pregnancy. The doctor told her to stop eating cake and sweets, and to take a walk every afternoon to Harris Promenade and back. He ordered Ma to rest for most of the day and avoid lifting anything heavy. The new routine didn't really affect Ma's daily schedule except for sewing; she loved to make herself and the girls beautiful dresses. Sewing was too strenuous, Dr Kroeh said, because she had to pedal the sewing machine and that could affect the baby. Sometimes, we put an ice pack on Ma's head and sometimes, a hot water bottle on her tummy. When the baby was due, the doctor took her to the hospital. The baby weighed ten pounds and Ma swore that was her last. So, Margaret got stuck with the name 'Baby' since there were no more babies after her.

James, my big brother, had passed the Senior Cambridge Examination and Pa asked Mr Bryan, a local solicitor in San Fernando, if James could work with him. Pa said if he could have afforded it, he would have sent James to England to pursue a degree in Law. I enjoyed working with Pa and I was so proud when the teachers spoke highly of him. He was definitely a model teacher for them. On mornings, Pa and I often walked ahead of Cynthia who had great difficulty climbing the hills of San Fernando. Every morning, she complained about walking to school.

'The exercise is good for you,' he told her. 'You're too young to be so fat. We can get a buggy to bring us home after school, but not in the morning,' he said.

'That's all right, Pa; I'll leave home early,' she assured him, but continued to bemoan her plight anyway.

Pa put Ben and Waldo in charge of the cow but they were always running away to play, causing Ma to routinely call their names aloud from the gallery. One Saturday, Ma made the mistake of sending Ben to buy fish on the wharf for the lunch meal. Myrtle had to go to Port of Spain on some urgent business, so Cynthia and I said we would help Ma cook – which meant I would be the one really helping Ma. Ben left at about eight o'clock; by eleven, he hadn't yet returned and by two in the afternoon, Pa got back home from school and started an intense search for Ben. We all joined in the manhunt. Ma had been collecting fibre from dried coconuts to make a small mattress and stored it in a huge box in the gallery. As she threw some more fibre into the box and pressed it down, she clutched a solid object and pulled up a head of hair. There was Ben fast asleep, while the whole household waited for him to return home with fish for lunch! Ma hit him on his head with the broom.

'Where's the money I gave you to buy fish?' she shouted at him.

'I spent it, Ma,' he whispered.

'On what?' she screamed.

'A slingshot,' he whispered again.

'A slingshot! Well, today your Pa going to make a slingshot out of you!' she threatened.

Pa tied Ben to a tree in the yard and gave him a solid thrashing with his leather belt.

One evening, when James returned home, he was brimming over with excitement about a Ford car he and Mr Bryan had seen in the newspaper. Unfortunately, we did not get to see the photograph. 'You sure that photo wasn't taken in England?' Ben teased him.

'I'm sure. Mr Bryan said it belongs to an English man drilling oil in America. Imagine, a Ford, and it cost about seven or eight hundred dollars,' James beamed.

'So you just have to dream about riding in that car, Cynthia,' Ben made a 'monkey face' at her.

'Even if I work for ten years I wouldn't be able to buy one,' moaned Cynthia. 'James, let's save up our money to buy one, even if it takes a few years,' she pleaded. 'I really can't take this walking anymore.'

'Sometime in the distant future, we will afford a car,' James dismissed the suggestion. 'I'm going to help Pa pay that house loan,' he promised.

'So what they doing with all the oil they drilling in Fyzabad – what they using that for?' asked Ben.

'They're refining it; that means they're treating it in a special way to use it as fuel for cars, ships and other engines. We wouldn't have to use so much coal and light coal pots again,' James said with authority.

'And how does the oil refinery in Trinidad change life for this grand household of ten?' questioned Cynthia, who was about to leave the room.

'It doesn't. We still have to keep walking, Cynthia – up the hill to La Pique,' I said, smiling. The school where she was teaching was built on a hill on the eastern side of the library corner.

Pa told us that Miss Bascum, one of his teachers at school, said her father was offered one thousand dollars for his land in Fyzabad, but when he spoke to Mr Bryan he was told not to sell. The land was valued much more than that because of the oil – something to do with oil rights.

'You see, James,' I said, 'these poor people in Fyzabad need a good lawyer to help them. Maybe when you qualify as a solicitor, you should go down there to work.'

He laughed. 'And dance cocoa in my spare time?' he mocked.

The following Sunday, while we were getting dressed to go to church, one of Ma's relatives-in-law, Auntie Beatrice, who lived on Harris Street, sent her daughter, Sheila, to ask Pa if there would be the usual morning church service.

'Ma said some friends from Oropouche pass home last night and say the Fyzabad oil well catch fire and explode, killing twenty people. Some of them were Sammys from Prince Alfred Street,' she informed us.

We were all shocked. Pa sent Waldo to ask Auntie Alice if she had heard the same news, but she hadn't. Pa said he was sure we would find out the truth if we went to church. Cynthia took Annette to Sunday school and the rest of the family went to midmorning service. At the end of service, Reverend Hall announced that several members of the Sammy family had perished in an oil explosion in Fyzabad and would be buried that same evening, following a funeral service at the church. As we were walking back home along Prince Alfred Street, a crowd of sympathisers assembled outside the Sammy residence. When we reached home, Aunt Indrani was waiting to see Pa.

'You too early for lunch, girl,' Pa said smiling. 'You start to go to church in San Fernando?'

'No, Bhai. Manwar and me come down to see de funeral. Beta know a boy from Princes Town who die in de fire, but dey didn't find de body. Well, dey not sure where Sam's body is.'

'So, where is Beta now?' Pa asked her.

'He went wit' Sam's mudder to de San Fernando hospital to find out if Sam's body is dere. Sam's family will meet she at de hospital, so Beta will come here afterwards. I sorry to bring such sad news, Bhai; I hope is not a bad sign,' she apologised.

Pa told us to go upstairs to change our clothes while

he spoke to Aunt Indrani. Ma asked me and Rose to help her with lunch, and Cynthia to keep an eye on Annette and the baby. From the kitchen, I could hear Pa telling Auntie and Uncle to stay for lunch, which they declined. Ma cut a piece of a huge sponge cake, which Myrtle had made and gave it to Auntie.

After lunch every Sunday, Ma and Pa settled into a siesta. Sunday afternoon was the only extended period of time you could be sure Pa stayed home. However, sometimes he would visit a sick member of the church or take a walk to Harris Promenade. This Sunday, the town was crowded as peopled flocked to the church grounds to witness the arrival of the funeral cortege. Pa said he would attend the funeral because Mr Sammy's father-in-law was one of the founders of the Susamachar church and an elder as well. When Pa left, Ben and Waldo asked to go to the cinema, but Ma said it was sure to be closed. As usual, Johnny was in his room working and Rose was studying for her nursing examination. Annette was playing with the neighbours' children in the street. The baby was sleeping and Ma, Cynthia and I went window-shopping on High Street. When Pa returned home that evening, he announced that Uncle Manwar was getting married to Saleema.

Pa, Cynthia and I attended Uncle Manwar's wedding. When we reached Uncle's house, he was waiting on Pa to accompany him to the Mosque. Cynthia took a cake for the wedding. She made it herself. Aunt Indrani quickly put it away on a high shelf in a kitchen cupboard. 'Just to make sure it didn't disappear,' she had said. The reception was to be held at Saleema's house, so we helped to pack a few pots of food and bottles of water in Uncle Manwar's donkey cart, and one of Saleema's brothers drove us to their home. A huge tent was built in the yard and covered with carat leaves. Long and short benches occupied the covered area and in one corner, several huge pots of food were placed on a table. Most of the guests were dressed in true Indian fashion except for Cynthia, me and Pa's two long-time friends, Jai and Gopee.

The wedding entourage returned from the Mosque and the *imam*, followed by Uncle Manwar and his bride, walked up the steps and into the house. Aunt Indrani held our hands and led us into the procession quickly before the crowd of guests followed. A short ceremony was performed and the couple was blessed. The guests took their gifts to the married couple and kissed them. Pa called us to come forward quickly to congratulate the newlyweds, after which Cynthia and I stood in the veranda and looked on curiously.

Saleema looked lovely in a bright yellow outfit, which fell to her ankles. Her veil was held in place by a jewelled headband. She wore a gold nose ring and wide silver bracelets. Uncle Manwar wore pale yellow long trousers and a matching embroidered *kurta* that reached below his knees. It was obvious that he was much older than Saleema but he did look very happy.

Pa introduced Cynthia and me to Auntie Deedee and Uncle Sayeed, whom he said were friends of his parents and were like godparents to him. Pa asked for Nath, Auntie Deedee's son, and was told he was studying to be a doctor in England. Both he and Khalim, Auntie Deedee's nephew, were abroad. Aunt Indrani left us to help serve food to the guests. At first,

Cynthia and I were surprised to see leaves used as plates but we managed fairly well. Finally, Aunt Indrani sat with us and I asked her why Uncle Manwar had decided to marry Saleema without giving the family adequate time to prepare for the wedding.

'Saleema's Bhap had a heart attack and the doctor said he cyah work as hard as he used to,' explained Auntie. 'So he think it best for her to get married before he get worse… or die.'

'And why, Uncle Manwar?' asked Cynthia.

'Well yuh see,' Auntie explained. 'Beta wanted to marry she for a long time now, but Saleema's Baap maybe feel dat Beta didn't have enough money den. So Beta jus' give up de whole idea.'

'Auntie, is Uncle Manwar rich now?' I asked her.

'I t'ink so, Beti, but I dohn know for sure how rich,' she answered.

After the welcome excitement of Uncle Manwar's wedding, Cynthia and I settled down to our routine of teaching and school-related activities. Pa said the church was organizing a meeting of Presbyterian schoolteachers and he wanted Cynthia and me to attend – even though we were inexperienced teachers.

'I hope we don't have to take the train to Couva, Pa,' Cynthia said.

'No, the teachers are meeting in San Fernando,' he replied.

'What's the purpose of the meeting?' she asked again.

'To discuss problems the schools may have and how to solve them, and to also give the teachers an opportunity to meet and know each other,' he explained.

'Are we meeting at the church Pa?' she asked again.

'No, Beti, at Grant School, but I'm sure we'll have a short service first.'

When Pa left the room, Cynthia said, 'I wonder if Pa is playing the matchmaker, Lily? You'll be first.'

'And you'll be next,' I teased.

'I don't think it ever crossed his mind,' Cynthia defended Pa.

'Don't let Pa fool you; he has eight children,' I reminded her. 'Don't underestimate your father's skill at intrigue; besides, we're getting old, you know.'

Before we went to the meeting, we discussed our apprehensions with Ma. 'Don't worry,' she consoled us. 'They'll have to pass my test first – and that will be difficult.'

A short service was conducted by Reverend Hall; then teachers and church officials proceeded to Grant School next door, where a full day's programme would materialise. Participants came from as far north as Couva and as far south as Penal. Jai and Gopee were there, of course. Pa was a guest speaker. He informed us of methods we should use in teaching children to read. He suggested using interesting Bible selections and stories from the Royal Reader, an English text we practically knew by heart, to hold the pupils' interest. Instead of insisting that parents, who were estate workers, buy slates for their infants, we could use sand until they were confident enough to use pencils and paper.

'Trust Pa to think of that,' whispered Cynthia. 'He should be in business, not teaching.'

Reverend Hall spoke about the success the

Ministers had achieved in spreading the religion and building new churches and schools, and in increasing the number of teachers being trained at the Naparima Teachers' Training College.

One catechist from Princes Town stressed the importance of Bible teaching in schools and organizing activities for the children to share Christian experiences together. Teachers were asked to volunteer to take charge of such groups as Boys' Scouts, TGIT church choirs and Bible study groups. Pa looked disappointed that Cynthia and I hadn't volunteered for any group – so finally, I joined the church choir and Cynthia the TGIT group leaders. After all the lecturing, we broke up into school groups and were introduced to each other by our head teachers. Pa knew everybody, but Cynthia and I light-heartedly scanned the crowd for eligible bachelors – handsome was definitely out of the question. Eventually, we gave up the search and were about to sneak out behind a blackboard when Pa emerged onto the stage looking left and right for someone or something.

'Lily, he's looking for us,' said Cynthia.

'Why you think so? Pa has his hands full now – all the people in the world he wants to talk to and he is where he is happiest.' I assured her.

'Then why isn't he talking to them and smiling? He's selected two gentlemen from the crowd and holding onto their shoulders. I think we should tell him we have to stay at home with Annette and Margaret for Ma. Come on Lily, let's go up front.' Cynthia pulled me along. We hurried up to the stage and told him we were leaving and why.

'Not so fast,' he said. 'I want you to meet two very well-respected teachers from Esperanza.'

'From where?' asked Cynthia.

'That's near Couva,' said one of the gentlemen.

Pa must be mad, I thought, and Ma would die if she knew what's happening here. Why would we be interested in anyone from Couva, much less Esperanza! They were both tall and well spoken, and were just beginning to develop receding hairlines. One was young and handsome, the other dark and in his late thirties or forty years old.

'This is Mr Andrew Lester and Mr Peter Ramdharry. Meet my daughters Lily and Cynthia.' We shook hands, mumbling brief pleasantries.

'Pa, we have to leave now; Ma wants us to come home early,' I said.

'Nice meeting you, Mr Lester; nice meeting you, Mr Ramdharry,' Cynthia and I echoed.

'What do you think?' I asked Cynthia as we strolled along Coffee Street.

'I'm not sure,' she said doubtfully. 'Mr Lester is certainly not Indian and the other gentleman seems quite preoccupied. They're both puzzles.'

Ma went out for a short while, but fortunately was back to play hostess when Pa brought Mr Lester home. I wondered what became of the other gentleman. They chatted for about an hour and Ma served some refreshments. Rose, Cynthia and I sat on the highest step of the staircase so that we would not be seen. It was difficult to hear what was being said downstairs in the living room, but we did understand enough to follow the proceedings. The conversation centred on schoolwork, pupils and school administration. Then, Mr Lester said it was time for him to leave; he was staying overnight in San Fernando at a relative's on Pointe-a-Pierre Road. Pa accompanied Mr Lester out of the house.

Rose and I tumbled down the stairs. 'What's the big secret meeting about, Ma?' Rose asked.

'It seems like he's an eligible bachelor interested enough to be coaxed into wedlock,' she announced.

Do I get to go out with him at least once before the big occasion, or is this an arranged marriage, I wondered.

'He's taking you to the cinema tomorrow at four,' Ma smiled. I could hardly believe my ears; Ma spoke as though she and Pa wanted me to get married and leave the household in a hurry.

Ma discovered that Mr Lester had two sisters, who lived with their mother in Arima. His father was a plantation overseer, but his parents were not married.

'And how is it he's Presbyterian?' I asked.

'It seems that his father had some connection with a minister who converted indentured workers and he went to school with their children.'

'So where's his father, Ma?' I asked.

'Maybe he went back to England or another island,' she said.

'Ma, is that a good thing or a bad thing?' I was getting quite concerned.

'What, Lily?'

'That he didn't really have a normal family – you know, that his father didn't live with them,' I added.

'Well I really can't say, my dear, but he seems to be

ambitious and also caring towards his mother and sisters. Besides, your Pa has an inclination towards him; maybe it's that male intuition. I would trust your Pa's judgment,' Ma reassured me.

One evening, we were about to go to bed and James hadn't arrived home yet. Ma started to get worried and Pa was at a church meeting.

'He said he would be late, Ma; he had to go to the Red House for Mr Bryan,' Rose said. 'I forgot to tell you, Ma.'

'The Red House was closed a long time ago. James is really going to Port of Spain often these days,' she commented. When Pa came home, James still hadn't arrived. Pa had a talk with him the next morning.

'You need to bring your friends home, son. Your mother and I want to meet them to ensure you're in good company – we are here to guide you,' he told James.

'Don't worry Pa. My friends are decent. I'm sure you and Ma will approve of them.' But, Ma was worried; she was sure a girl was involved. As we hardly ever saw James, and he was the only person in the house with his own room, we couldn't really have good communication with him. James didn't confide in anyone at home. Occasionally, he would give Rose a message for Ma if he had to leave early or come home late. Ma asked Pa to talk to James again. Instead, Pa visited Mr Bryan in his office one day when James went to Port of Spain.

'How often does he go to the Red House for you?' Pa asked Mr Bryan.

'Not more than once a week, Mr Sanowar – that's a

very long journey,' he said. 'I suspect he has made friends in Port of Spain – a young lady in particular, a barrister's daughter.'

Ma was so upset that she quarrelled with James for not being honest with her and Pa after all they had sacrificed for him. James was not much of a talker by nature, but he admitted to Ma that he was thinking of getting married to a lady in Port of Spain.

'That is no lady!' Ma screamed at him, 'If she and her parents were decent and respectful, they wouldn't encourage you like they want to kidnap you!'

'Don't say that, Ma,' James pleaded. 'Her father is a lawyer and a respectable man in Port of Spain.'

'And you've been to their house, I imagine.'

'Yes, twice,' he admitted.

'And not one word until now,' she complained, 'until I force it out of you.'

Pa made arrangements for James' wedding ceremony at the church and we all attended, but we didn't see too much of him after that. He went to live in Port of Spain.

Ma was despondent for a long time after James left home, so Cynthia promised to have a telephone installed so that Ma could talk to James. Rose wrote her nursing examinations and was awarded a scholarship to go to Canada. She was so excited about going away, but Ma was not thrilled.

'I'm happy for you, Rose, but I think you're really brave. You really want to live in the cold?' Ma asked her.

'I'll think of that when I get there. Don't worry, Ma – we all have to make our own lives and I want to be a good, qualified nurse,' she said. Pa was excited too, but as usual, he tried not to show it. Ma was the opposite; she burst into tears at the thought of all her children leaving the house.

'We're not all leaving you, Ma,' Cynthia consoled her. 'I'll be here for a long time now that James is gone. Pa needs help with that loan.'

Ben and Waldo were inseparable. Ma said a fly couldn't pass between them. Ben hated studying and Pa had to help him with his schoolwork. He couldn't sit still for long and sometimes, Pa used his leather belt to do the talking. Eventually, Ben passed his Junior Cambridge Examination, and Ma said before Pa killed him with thrashings, he should leave school and look for a job. But Pa persisted in encouraging Ben to keep working at his lessons. At last he was able to find him a job at a pharmacy, so Ben left school and started learning to be a pharmacist.

Waldo turned out to be a sickly child and often, he retreated to bed with a terrible cold. At one time, Ma said it might be tuberculosis, but Dr Kroel told Ma not to worry. He would outgrow the symptoms. Thanks to Rose, Waldo was able to get the prescribed medication. But, there were times when drugs were unavailable and it looked like Ma was losing her mind, worrying about Waldo.

Pa brought up the subject of marriage, and it seemed a foregone conclusion that I had accepted Andrew Lester's proposal. Ma worked on my wedding dress for two weeks and Cynthia paid Aunt Alice's seamstress to make dresses for all the ladies in the family, including Ma.

One Saturday afternoon, one month before the selected date, Pa and I went to Princes Town to invite Uncle Manwar, Aunt Saleema and Aunt Indrani to my wedding. They were delighted to see us. Uncle said he had given up growing cocoa and had started a buggy service to San Fernando. He was hoping to save enough money to invest in a bus service in the near future. Aunt Indrani looked well but she had aged much more quickly than Pa, even though she was only two years older than he.

A date was set for my wedding and my parents discussed their plans behind closed doors. Times were difficult and money was scarce. Most wedding celebrations were usually quite modest because World War II had resulted in severe food shortages. Communication was limited, and even the recently introduced telephone system was unreliable. Amid all these difficult conditions, life continued with an adjusted normalcy.

Andrew and I got married at the Susamachar Church in San Fernando. Ma made my dress and it was beautiful. Waldo was the ring bearer, and Annette and Margaret were flower girls. Rose and Cynthia were bridesmaids. Both Ma and Pa looked pleased with themselves, and while James and his wife attended the ceremony at the church, they left soon after. We had a small reception at home and I couldn't help but burst into tears before Andrew and I left for Couva. I knew I would miss my parents and the children, but most of all, I would miss Cynthia.

Pa was instrumental in getting me a transfer to the same school where Andrew and also Mr Ramdharry taught. We lived in Couva though, transportation being more available from there along the Southern Main Road. Mr Ramdharry was a close friend of Andrew's, although older than him by about ten years. He was a widower, his wife having died in childbirth, and was left with four children and a sister who lived with him – until she got married. Pa said he had met him twice before the teachers' convention, which Cynthia and I had attended, but didn't really know him well.

'He's an excellent teacher,' Andrew told Pa one day when he visited us. 'He's very involved in his work and the welfare of the students.'

Pa suggested he and Andrew visit Mr Ramdharry's home as he wanted to see him in his context. Pa was impressed. Mr Ramdharry had a comfortable house in a very convenient location. He had four children, the youngest about three or four and the eldest about ten.

'Who takes care of the children, Pa?' I asked.

'His sister, and sometimes a helper as well,' he answered indifferently. Pa was more interested in Mr Ramdharry's status in the community than his domestic situation. I knew he was getting anxious about Cynthia being single. She had recently celebrated her thirty-fourth birthday. We needed another opinion on this subject, so when Pa left, I telephoned Ma from one of Andrew's friends' home.

'Hello Ma, how're you keeping?' I asked.

'Fine,' she said. 'My sugar level is under control.'

'Pa just left here; he and Andrew visited Mr Ramdharry at his home. Pa seems pleased with what he saw,' I informed her.

'Your Pa must be dreaming he's in India, Lily. That

man is getting old and panicking that Cynthia may end up as an old maid,' she stormed. 'My daughter can do without that kind of arranged marriage. Cynthia isn't anxious to get married, at least not to a widower with four children.'

'Ma, you need to invite Mr Ramdharry to assess him yourself, you know – the kind of person he is. Cynthia is a kind and generous person and you need to find out if she can deal with the situation. Don't tell Pa I spoke to you. I have to go now; I'm using a friend's 'phone. Take care of yourself.' I was worried and I knew that Ma was too.

Ma said she thanked God every Sunday at church for helping Ben settle down into a job he seemed to like. He enjoyed mixing various concoctions for patients who came to the pharmacy where he worked. Sometimes when he got home, Ma said Ben was so enthusiastic about his job that she wondered what sinister plan he was devising. Pa encouraged him to keep studying for his examinations and when the results were released, he was successful. Pa said he would help him open his own pharmacy, but before he could do that Ben brought home a young lady. Ma was stunned and Ben was almost tongue-tied.

The rainy season had just begun and it was Ma's custom to plant her Christmas shrubs in September. One afternoon, Waldo was helping Ma prepare the soil for planting, when Ben and a young lady entered the front walkway.

'Good afternoon, Ma,' he greeted her.

'You're early today,' Ma said. 'Is something wrong?'

'Oh, no! Mr Bentley gave us some time off – he

closed the pharmacy because he had to go to a funeral,' he explained.

'And are you going to introduce me to your friend?' Ma inquired.

'Oh! Yes, Ma. This is Deborah; she works at the pharmacy too. We're going to the cinema this afternoon. Is Pa home yet?' he asked.

'No – not yet. He'll be late today. He's giving extra lessons to students writing examinations. What movie are you going to see?' Ma asked.

'*Bridge on the River Kwai*,' Deborah replied.

'At which cinema?' Ma asked again.

'New Cinema,' she answered.

'Where do you live, Deborah?' It was Ma's habit to interrogate all newcomers to the household to ensure her children were in good company.

'Port of Spain. Mr Bentley is my uncle-in-law, so it was easy to get a job at his pharmacy,' she explained.

'So you stay with him during the week?' Ma asked.

'Yes, and on some weekends, I go to Port of Spain,' she added. Ben began to twitch the front of his shoes as though his toes were itching.

'Okay, run along then before it's too late for your show, and try to get home early,' she cautioned.

They bumped into each other as they hurried into the street.

Sometimes, Pa and Cynthia visited us on Saturdays. Usually Andrew and Pa wandered off towards the church on the Main Road, which offered some weekend activity. I could tell that Pa was attracted to the area; it probably reminded him of his childhood when he first came to Trinidad.

One Saturday, in particular, Cynthia brought Margaret with her. I was sixteen years older than Margaret, our 'Baby', so we certainly didn't have much in common, but Cynthia showed fondness for her. They looked so much alike – fat, fair and cheerful characters, always chatting and filling their stomachs. Everybody spoiled Margaret – Cynthia, Ma, even Pa sometimes. I remember that at Vistabella, Pa would let her sleep on a makeshift bed of school benches after school, while he put his schedule in order for the next day. Cynthia hated housework, but she often baked and brought Andrew and me a cake.

'What's happening at school these days?' I asked her. She was teaching at Naparima Girls' High School.

'Oh, the usual,' she replied. 'But, I'm planning a trip to Los Iros for the TGIT group.'

'To the beach! Will the school allow that?' I was surprised.

'Oh, yes. Some of the teachers are going too, and Margaret. Miss Dyal's brother owns a bus – so we'll all be a happy school family,' she boasted.

'What about Annette?' I wondered if she was being left out.

'Oh, she's not very interested; she prefers to go to the cinema with Ma in the afternoon.'

'How are you doing at school, Margaret?' I asked. I knew she and Annette did poorly. They didn't have to work hard because Ma gave them anything they asked for and Cynthia had her seamstress make beautiful clothes for them all the time.

'I hate school,' she answered shamelessly. 'Especially Religious Study. Mrs Hall complained to Pa that I didn't know where Jesus was born.'

'Well, you should know that at least,' I scolded her.

Cynthia said that Ma received a letter from Rose, who was studying in Canada. She mentioned meeting a young man from San Fernando in Toronto; his name is Jamal Hosein.

'A Muslim?' I was surprised. 'Is she really interested in him?'

'Ma said she seemed excited about him,' Cynthia answered.

'I wonder what Pa would say about that!' Pa was Muslim before he became a Christian.

'Did Ma tell you about the Ben-Deborah encounter?' I asked Cynthia.

She laughed. 'Can you imagine? Ben, of all people!' she exclaimed

'Ma was a little worried though,' Margaret commented. 'She said Ben has this strange way of going off and doing things by himself. Remember when he left school and went to swim off the jetty, and when Pa ran into him window-shopping during school hours?' she added.

'Poor Ben, he never liked school; Pa did the best he could for him,' said Cynthia.

'Do you realise Pa doesn't have time for the boys? I'm not blaming him; he's always so busy, but you don't expect them to stay at home and chat with Ma, do you? James ran off the same way and found a lady of his choice. And so did Pa,' I added. We laughed.

When Andrew and Pa returned from their outing, they were full of 'male chatter'. They were discussing the latest developments in the oil industry. Pa said a new political party had been formed by Uriah Butler, a Grenadian who had immigrated to Trinidad earlier on. He had mobilised the oil workers in a bid for better wages. The British were making a fortune in the oil industry and oil was being refined at Pointe-a-Pierre. There was a strike on the waterfront in Port of Spain and several trade unions were being established in the main town of the island.

'It's a pity nobody can bargain for the East Indian farmers,' Pa said. 'Their conditions haven't changed in the least, for decades.'

'Thanks to history, Pa, our society is not concerned about all of our people,' added Andrew.

One Saturday, Andrew and I were pleasantly surprised by Ma's visit. Cynthia came with her. Ma said that Ben told her and Pa that he wanted to marry Deborah.

'Actually,' Ma said. 'He disclosed his heart's desire to your Pa on their way home after work, and Pa insisted that the three of us discuss the matter. He wants to live at home for a while after they're married,' she added.

'How do you feel about the wedding, Ma?' I asked.

'I was so angry that I was speechless,' she raised her voice. 'Imagine your Pa and I are making plans to help him organise his own pharmacy, when big man like him announces he's getting married.'

'How does Pa feel about Ben's partner?' I asked.

'That was another surprise – he approved. He was delighted for them to live with us for a while, until they could afford to get a place of their own,' she exhaled.

'What did Pa say about Ben marrying a non-Indian?' I asked.

'Nothing, absolutely nothing. I don't object to that decision, really – but he never even brought Deborah home and introduced her properly to us,' she complained.

'Ma,' Cynthia stalled her, 'maybe he was afraid you would disapprove of her and he didn't want you to cross examine her.'

'Why not?' Ma fumed. 'It's my duty to know my children's marriage partners, so that I can guide them. Now, that's a second son keeping his distance and I don't like it,' she concluded.

Andrew and I attended the wedding ceremony at the Susamachar church and afterwards, Ma had a small reception at home. Then, Ben and Deborah disappeared for two days in traditional style. Ma said she hardly ever saw them, except in the evening, before she retired to bed. They occupied James' former room, the front bedroom.

The local newspaper reported that the war in Europe had rekindled American interest in the Caribbean. It was said that the Americans were building naval bases and airstrips in several islands in the Caribbean, including Trinidad. The unemployed flocked to Chagaramas and Arima looking for jobs, and land was being sold on the outskirts of Port of Spain in an effort to develop the area.

The Americans were also building a highway out of Port of Spain. This meant that an extensive residential area was being developed towards the north and south of the new highway, the Eastern Main Road. Andrew and I decided to purchase a house lot and move to Barataria. There were no Presbyterian schools in that area, so Andrew said he would apply for a post which had become vacant on the Presbyterian Board of Managers. I decided to retire from the teaching service, when I realised that I was having my first baby.

Annette and Margaret started visiting us in Barataria, and we were able to introduce them to several of our newly made friends in our neighbourhood. In spite of the war, there was quite a bit of activity in the area of entertainment. My sisters often enjoyed themselves and stayed over with Andrew and me. Annette had written her examinations and left Secondary school. Unfortunately, Ma developed diabetes after years of commendable health. Her doctor put her on a special diet and Ma asked Margaret to leave school to stay home with her. Pa retired the following year, having attained the age of sixty-five, and Ben and Deborah moved out of the family house to a rented apartment.

Pa's school had a grand retirement celebration for him. The teachers presented him with a lovely silver watch, which he really didn't need then – but which Ma said he was sure to make good use of anyway. Ma was present, for a change. Usually, she did not like to attend these lengthy events, but she wanted to support Pa on his special occasion. After all, she claimed it might have been her last visit to the school. All Pa's children, except James, attended the function. The pupils sang nostalgic songs and hymns, and the teachers' eyes were tear-filled. He had worked hard for fifty-one years and had been the schoolmaster at

Vistabella for forty years. At our church, Pa was made an elder for life. The missionaries recognised that the schoolmasters had played a crucial role in educating students as well as imparting Christian principles to them. Without the help of the early converts, they could not have hoped to succeed in teaching Christianity to the large numbers of children who attended their schools. For his undying faith and dedication, Pa was honoured by being selected to represent one of the twelve disciples, whom Jesus had chosen to walk in His footsteps. Pa was elated. He would have to serve communion every first Sunday in the month, collect the offering at all the services he attended, visit the sick and become a member of certain church committees.

'At last, he could have a good rest,' I said to Ma.

'Keep your fingers crossed,' she said. 'This may just be a full-time job.'

As soon as Pa had enjoyed one week's vacation, he started working on opening a pharmacy for Ben. They rented a small ground floor structure on Coffee Street and Pa was self-employed as a part-time, voluntary worker. Months later, Pa was rewarded with a grandson.

Andrew and I often visited Ma, now that she was unable to travel. Some days, she would stay in bed for a few hours, but always walked to Harris Promenade and back on afternoons. Pa enjoyed his new occupation. Margaret was at Ma's 'beck and call' and Cynthia was the only member of the family who had a full-time job. Waldo said that Pa was negotiating the purchase of a portion of agricultural land in Debe on his behalf. Many sugar-cane peasant farmers were selling out completely or selling part of their property, and moving on to producing cash crops.

'What kind of crops are you thinking of growing, Waldo?' I asked.

'Citrus,' he said.

'That's new,' I commented.

'Brand new – there's a great demand for citrus now that the town has such a large population. I think a local company is thinking of producing canned fruit juice,' he informed me. He prided himself on knowing a great deal about agriculture. It must be in the blood, I thought. He's the first in this family to show such an interest.

The war had started and Trinidad experienced a severe economic depression. Prices increased and foodstuff was in limited supply and had to be rationed. Even communication was affected; transportation was dependable only during working hours.

Ma said she had received a telephone call from Mr Ramdharry requesting a meeting with her and Pa on the following Saturday. She selected a time when Cynthia was usually involved with the TGIT group and when the house was fairly quiet. Pa, Ma and Margaret were at home when Mr Ramdharry arrived.

Margaret made a hasty exit as the visitor was invited to sit in the living room, but reserved a position on the top of the staircase, far out of sight. She was able to recognise the speakers from their voices, Ma's being the most forceful and slightly aggressive; Pa's was encouraging and Mr Ramdharry's, very matter of fact. He conveyed his intentions, that he was interested in getting married to Cynthia, and said he would request a transfer from the school board on her behalf. Pa said he would work on that, and Cynthia and Pa planned to visit Mr Ramdharry the following Saturday.

Ma said she had the strangest feeling in her stomach after Mr Ramdharry left. She felt as though she had just crashed into a stone wall.

'You're overreacting, Anna,' Pa said to her.

'Mothers have a special intuition about each of their children, McKenzie,' Ma always addressed Pa as such when she was angry. 'This one is not for Cynthia. Our daughter is a kind, open-hearted, loving person. Why are we doing this to her?' she asked Pa.

'Doing what, Anna?' Pa sounded confused. 'I'm just trying to prevent her from living a very lonely life. When we are dead and gone what will become of her?'

'I'm not ready to die yet,' retorted Ma.

'I know that, Anna, but we have to help Cynthia now. We can't wait for when it's too late – she is over thirty years old. Do you want her to end up like my sister? Her companions are chickens and sheep and goats!' Pa concluded.

Ma was silent.

When Pa and Cynthia returned from their visit to Mr Ramdharry's, the wedding date was announced. Pa made arrangements for the ceremony to be held at the San Fernando church. Andrew and I arrived a few minutes before the organ music started. It was a beautiful, simple ceremony. Annette and Margaret were bridesmaids and Ben's little son, now five years old, was the ring bearer. Pa looked pleased with himself, but Ma's eyes welled up with tears. There was a small reception at the family house which turned out to be a delightful family reunion. Andrew and I stayed overnight and left the next morning for Barataria. Pa said that Peter and Cynthia would spend a few days in Los Iros before going to Couva.

Ten months after Cynthia's wedding, she gave birth to a baby girl. Ma and Margaret visited them regularly, and Margaret often stayed for a few days to help look after the baby while Cynthia was at work.

Andrew and I stopped by one Saturday morning on our way to San Fernando. Peter and the children had gone to the market and Margaret was spending the weekend.

'How're you coping with the ready-made family and your job, Sis?' I asked.

'It's a little more than I can manage, I must admit, but I'm trying,' she answered.

'Does Peter help?' I pried.

'Oh, yes, Lily. In all fairness to him, he does as much as he can, but he's also very involved in his work. He loves his children a lot,' she answered.

'So that leaves very little time for you,' I assumed.

'We are all so very busy, my dear; we don't have time to be sorry for ourselves,' she rationalised.

'You look well, though,' I observed. 'In the pink of health.'

One year later, Cynthia gave birth to a second baby girl, but she was stillborn. The doctor advised her to remain at the hospital and Margaret took the baby, Jen, home to San Fernando. Ma wanted Cynthia to return home for a while, but Cynthia's doctor said it would be dangerous for her to travel. So Pa and Margaret visited Cynthia as often as they could and took items to her, which were in short supply. One month after she was hospitalised, Cynthia died. After that, Ma was confined to bed and Pa stayed at home more often.

CHAPTER 5

My Heritage

Bespectacled and grey,
Gently rocking in his chair
Poring o'er the printed word,
Seeking knowledge was his care.
Old, retired, widowed, wan,
Alone, but never lonely:
The written word, the music note
Was all it took to cheer him.
A traveller from a former time
Another place, another land.
A memory dimmed, a lifetime
    lived
A heritage of pride.
'This is my home, this, my child
Is yours to have and treasure.
The world is always changing,
Time hastens on to meet
The challenge of the future
And knowledge from defeat.
The future lies with progress
Travel on with Time
God's love can never fail –
His gift to all Mankind.'

'Good morning, Grandma, can I come up and lie next to you?' I asked.

'Come on up, Jen.' She kissed me on my forehead and pulled me up on her bed, her arm encircling my tiny body.

'And how is my little granddaughter this morning?' she enquired.

'Still sleepy – mosquitoes got into the net. Where's Grandpa? He's not upstairs.'

'He went to the shop to get a few items for me, but he'll be back soon,' she assured me.

'Did you have breakfast yet?' I asked.

'No, not yet. Auntie Margaret is bringing it up in a while – she went downstairs to the kitchen.'

My grandmother stayed in bed most of the day, but was still strong enough to take an occasional stroll to the promenade, make a cup of tea in the pantry upstairs and attend to her personal hygiene. She seldom ventured downstairs, except late in the afternoon to sit and chat with Grandpa in the living room or to admire her flowers in the front garden. On evenings, she would stand in the gallery to inhale the perfume exuding from her 'ladies of the night' that lined the street pavement. Grandma loved flowers. The front portion of the yard was adorned with red and yellow cannas, pink and white roses, a tall prickly cactus that flowered annually and a variety of ferns. In the gallery adjacent to her bedroom, hung huge circular wire baskets filled with black-speckled, moss-green ferns, which offered perpetual shade and comfort. Her bedroom was the largest in the house and I loved to lie in her bed and comb her hair or pretend I was using the phone attached to the wall, too high for me to reach. She enjoyed having children around her. My cousin Gillian lived downstairs with her parents; she was Aunt Annette's daughter. Her father had been an army officer, but since the war ended he had had several different jobs. Grandma often played 'dolly house' with us and gave us real money to pretend we had a shop. We kept a collection of farthings and cents, but pennies were too valuable a commodity for play. We usually dropped these in the offering plates at church. Sometimes, when the rain poured heavily outside, Gillian and I would cuddle on either side of my grandmother and smother ourselves and her face with the blanket. One thunderous, stormy day we were so terrified by flashes of forked lightning and repeated, crashing peals of thunder that we fled to the bathroom and into the shower with her. Grandma enjoyed being part of our childish fun, but often we were scooted off by my grandfather, who had no time for empty indulgences.

I loved living on Gordon Street. The presence of grandparents who stayed at home offered a warm and protective luxury. The spacious, old, wooden house with several rooms – large and small, echoed untold tales of former occupants, their photographs in black and white, enhanced by heavy, embossed frames displaying serious and pensive faces. The huge painting of a brown and white cow seated comfortably in a flowing stream beneath a windmill was part of my childhood and belonged to that house. It was the creation of a great aunt, my grandmother's sister, who had lived in the countryside and who had died a long time ago.

Grandpa reminded us that the fruit trees were

treasures. He forbade us to climb any of them since they were planted in honour of the birth of his children.

'Which is your favourite, Grandpa?' I asked him one day.

'All, I like them all – they make the yard complete and remind me of the times when each of my children was born. They help me to relive a very cherished period of time,' he replied.

On afternoons when the neighbours' children came home from school, we played in the street until dark. Dawn and Debbie from next door, Jim and Terrance who lived opposite to us, and Gillian and I owned that street.

'You are all wasting precious time playing silly games,' Grandpa scolded, 'when you could be reading and working sums.' We tried to ignore him. We enjoyed playing childhood games like 'Umbrella Spin' and spun around from the top of the hill to the bottom, until we grew giddy and fell, or dropped out of the race. 'Traffic Lights', we knew in our imaginary world, but not in reality until much later in life. The war taught us to be soldiers in the game, 'Germans and English.' We dared to be Germans to give the other nation, the opposing team, a grand thrashing when caught. On rainy days, we made little boats from popsicle sticks, wrote our names on them and raced them in the shallow drain, speeding headlong behind, to watch as they fell helplessly into the 'canal' at the bottom of the street. When we crept indoors, soaking wet, Grandpa was sure to be awaiting our arrival. But on most occasions, Gillian and I managed to dodge the sharp sting of his leather belt and hid under Grandma's bed.

Grandma had been asking Grandpa to go to the beach at Los Iros for a few days, so the whole family went further south on a short holiday. The adults spent most of the day bathing in the sea and chatting, while Gillian and I explored a coconut plantation nearby. We collected dried coconuts, water coconuts and baby coconut plants to take home. Grandpa spent most of the day helping my grandmother move around and making her comfortable.

Two days after we returned home, my grandmother fell ill again. The doctor ordered her to stay in bed. He visited every morning and gave her a penicillin injection from a small bottle with a blue wrapper. Sometimes, Aunt Margaret would have to get her the hot water bottle, and sometimes the ice pack. Every morning, the ice truck delivered a huge block of ice and the milkman left two bottles of milk on the front step. Aunt Margaret looked after my grandmother during the day, and Myrtle made special fish and chicken broth which was given to her in a feeding cup. At night Nurse Strome sat in the rocking chair watching her all night. She placed a purple lampshade around the light in Grandma's room. Gillian and I were unable to lie with her and play funny games anymore. Her room was out of bounds to us.

One afternoon, when Gillian and I were reading a storybook upstairs in Grandpa's bed, Aunt Margaret called us downstairs. We confronted a tall, brown-skinned, straight-haired gentleman.

'Do you know who this is?' Aunt Margaret asked us.

'No, Auntie,' we chorused.

'This is your Uncle James; he came to see your grandmother,' continued Aunt Margaret.

'Good afternoon, Uncle James,' we chorused again as he held our hands and smiled.

'Ma isn't well at all, James. Dr Kroel said she's taken a turn for the worse. Pa keeps telling her she'll be well soon, but Ma doesn't talk much,' disclosed Aunt Margaret in a whisper. 'Run along, children – you can go outside and play now,' she shouted to me and Gillian. We walked out of the room slowly.

'Who's paying all the bills?' asked James.

'Pa, of course. Sometimes, Ben brings some medication, but it's difficult to get drugs nowadays, you know, since the war. Maybe you can offer to help. He's not wealthy you know.' She reminded him of his duty, often forgotten.

While Grandma was bedridden, relatives we hadn't seen for a long time visited – Aunt Lily and Uncle Andrew from Barataria, Uncle Manwar, his wife, Aunt Saleema and Aunt Indrani from Princes Town, Grandma's sister, Aunt Alice, Aunt Chokoon, Uncle Harvey Aaron who lived two streets away, and the neighbours, who came almost everyday.

One day after lunch, I fell asleep in Grandpa's bed and when I woke up there was no one upstairs. I looked in Grandma's room, but she wasn't there. I hoped they hadn't left me home alone, I thought. Everyone was standing in the living room staring at a long grey metal box on legs, covered with beautiful white lilies.

'Where's Grandma?' I asked Aunt Margaret.

'Not so loud,' said Gillian. 'Grandma got very ill and had to go away,' she said.

'Are those flowers for her?' I asked again.

'Yes, they are for her,' Aunt Margaret answered and took me outside with the other children. The next day, we all got dressed. Gillian and I wore white dresses. Gillian's Mom and Aunt Margaret wore black, and Grandpa and Gillian's dad wore dark-coloured suits. We followed a slow-moving vehicle to the Church and the Minister conducted a service. Afterwards, Myrtle took me home and we never saw Grandma again.

My first writing lesson occurred on the beach. Every morning, Grandpa and I would walk along the sandy seafront and write capital letters in the sand. The area was not popular for sea bathing. There were huge rocks in some places, in an area was named Flat Rock and usually, only strong swimmers frequented that portion of the beach.

When I was five, I began to attend the San Fernando Anglican Infant School on Harris Promenade, which was a short walking distance from our home. Sometimes, Grandpa would take me to school in the mornings, and in the afternoons, I was accompanied by a friend of the family, Thelma, who took her niece to the same school. We wrote on slates with slate pencils that made squeaking noises. When writing classes ended, Miss Atherley stored the slates and pencils in her cupboard. Gillian attended the Anglican Primary School on the southern side of the town. In the mornings, we raced each other to see who would reach the top of the hill first, I to the north and she, to the south of Gordon Street.

Grandpa gave us lessons on afternoons. In the evening, we read the newspapers and at night, we read three chapters from the Bible. We knelt at Grandpa's bedside to pray for all the people dear to us and to ask the Heavenly Father for guidance in our lives.

When I turned six, I began attending Grant School and Grandpa went to Uncle Ben's pharmacy every day. He helped to sell patent medicines and gave Uncle Ben's children lessons when they arrived there after school. The pharmacy was now on Mucurapo Street, an extremely busy market street. Grandpa enjoyed meeting his 'old time' friends, who came there from Princes Town, Debe and Penal. He often spoke in Hindi and bowed '*Salaam*' to them. When they were unable to explain what they needed from the pharmacy, Grandpa translated in English for Uncle Ben. Busy market days made him happy and drove his loneliness away. He was particularly fond of Uncle Ben's eldest child, Omar, whom he insisted was working towards an island scholarship. After school, I would meet him at the pharmacy and we would walk through Paradise Cemetery on our way home.

In San Fernando, the celebration of India's Independence was not to be ignored. A huge life-size statue of Mahatma Gandhi was erected and occupied a prominent position on Harris Promenade. A garlanding ceremony was held to honour the Indian hero. People from all over Trinidad attended to celebrate not only their ancient homeland's victory, but their own independence now that the British islands had been granted universal adult suffrage. This was a measure of freedom at last; they were no longer bound to the sugar or cocoa plantations. Muslim and Hindu marriages were also recognised in Trinidad, and local Indian associations were contemplating building elementary and secondary schools for Hindu and Muslim children.

Often, on afternoons, I accompanied my grandfather on a leisurely walk, which invariably ended with our sitting under a huge flamboyant tree on Harris Promenade. The police band performed in the bandstand once or twice weekly, while children danced and played on the grass. This was a recreational as well as a historic site. Old colonial churches dominated the landscape; several religions were represented – Anglicans, Roman Catholics and Methodists. At the eastern end of the promenade was my favourite rendezvous, the Carnegie Free Library, where my friends and I spent hours – especially during the holidays – browsing through volumes of children's picture books and selecting reading material that we borrowed to take home. We were safe here and were allowed to stay as long as we liked, provided that we left for home before the town became busy with workers leaving their offices and business places for the day.

One thing Gillian and I disliked about Grandpa was that he never wasted a single minute. One afternoon, we were sitting on the benches and enjoying the cool easterly breezes on the Promenade and he promptly initiated a lesson in time telling. The big, bold black numbers on the Roman Catholic Church clock naturally attracted attention.

'What time is it now Gillian?' he asked.

'Twenty – past five,' she answered.

'Incorrect. It is exactly twenty-one minutes past five o'clock,' he pointed an unwavering forefinger at her. He continued the lesson for the next ten minutes. Then, Gillian said she wanted to run across the street for some water and left.

'Have you ever been to the Catholic Church, Grandpa?' I asked him.

'No, never,' he answered abruptly.

'Why can't we go there sometimes, and why can't I go to the school here, so close to home?' I asked again.

'Because we are not Roman Catholics; we are Presbyterians – so you must attend the school which teaches your religion,' he explained.

'Aren't we all Christians, believing in Jesus and God, and going to church on Sunday?' I persisted.

'You see, Beti,' he cleared his throat, before explaining to me, 'certain Canadian ministers built our churches for us – people like me who came from India and their children, and grandchildren. The Roman Catholic church was built for the Spanish and French people who came to Trinidad a very long time ago – long before I was born.'

So whenever I walked along the promenade towards the library, and passed the Roman Catholic Church on my left and St Joseph's Convent on my right, I stared directly ahead.

Weekends lost the fun and excitement I had experienced when Grandma was alive. Gillian and I still played in the street, although I played a lot more than her, especially at school where we pitched marbles and played 'rounders' and 'Hopscotch' at lunchtime. On Saturdays, we went to the Carnegie Library to borrow books and watch the puppet shows. On Sundays, I went to Sunday school and sang in the choir, then attended Sunday service with Grandpa who came later on. He was getting old and when he stood at the front of the church and received the heavy silver server, which held tiny glasses of grape juice for the congregation at Holy Communion, I shuddered to wonder if he was too feeble to carry it. But, it never fell.

Sometimes, Uncle Waldo brought Grandpa oranges and grapefruits, and Uncle Andrew visited too, while Aunt Lily invited him repeatedly to come to Barataria. One Saturday morning, we took the train to Port of Spain, where we arrived at two in the afternoon. Aunt Lily and Uncle Andrew met us at the train station and in the evening, we went to the Travelling Circus at Queen's Park Savannah. It was the first time that I saw and ate cotton candy. 'How much does this cost?' Grandpa asked the cotton candy man.

'Twelve cents, Sir,' he replied.

'The price of an exercise book,' he commented to our embarrassment.

One December, just before Christmas, Aunt Rose visited us from Canada. I didn't know her in person and had to be introduced.

'Hi, Jen,' she smiled. 'I'm Auntie Rose, your godmother. I brought you this doll.' I had never known I had a godmother.

'Give Auntie Rose a kiss and say thanks, Jen,' Aunt Margaret insisted. She was hardly ever around lately, and she and Grandpa often argued about something or the other.

'Thank you, Auntie,' I said.

'And how are you, Dad?' she addressed Grandpa. 'You look fine, although you need to put on some weight. I'm really so happy to be here,' she said, as she spun around surveying the familiar old house and its fixtures. 'It really feels like home,' she said, but she didn't spend her holiday with us and Grandpa was disappointed.

My Birthday Book made provision for seven birthdays and since I had never had a birthday party in my whole life, Aunt Margaret insisted that she and Grandpa invite my friends for my seventh birthday. She and Myrtle made the prettiest cake I had ever seen. We had fruit punch, candies and ice cream. Gillian and I tied balloons and hung them in the living room, and Aunt Margaret spread out Grandma's pretty, white crocheted table cloth on the dining room table. Dawn and Debbie, Jim and Terrence, some of Gillian's school friends and Uncle Waldo's two daughters, Tess and Flora all came.

It was a beautiful afternoon, which meant we could play outside after the indoor festivities. When my guests arrived, wished me a happy birthday, kissed me and filled my arms with beautifully wrapped presents, I was overjoyed. Aunt Margaret played a Happy Birthday record on the old gramophone and called the children to stand around the table, where the birthday cake glowed with lighted candles.

'Get ready to blow out the candles, Jen, all together now,' she reminded me and started a chorus of the birthday song. She blindfolded me and asked me to select a partner to cut the cake. Jim was the lucky one. He greedily shoved a half slice of cake into his mouth and forced himself to chew and swallow it.

All this time, I hardly realised that Grandpa was not a part of the activities. He was seated near the window reading his newspaper.

'Aunt Margaret, aren't we going to include him in the party?' I asked.

'He is in the party, Jen, but he's too old for all this. I'll give him a piece of cake and a drink in a while,' she assured me.

When we had stuffed ourselves silly with all the goodies, Aunt Margaret arranged the chairs on the veranda for us to play musical chairs. We played 'Pin the Donkey Tail' and 'Hopscotch', pitched marbles and played hoop with Terrence's dog. We sang to musical games, 'Here We Go Round the Mulberry Bush,' 'Drop Peter Drop' and 'In a Fine Castle'.

The children were exhausted, so we all went back inside to have cool drinks and devour the sweets. Grandpa was setting up a classroom scenario. 'Bring out the blackboard and chalk, Jen,' he called. 'It's time for the children to catch their breath and do some serious thinking.' I couldn't believe what was happening. The music on the gramophone screeched to a stop and silence reigned. My friends were horrified; they stared as if they had seen a ghost.

'Is this the end of the party, Jen?' whispered Dawn.

'Oh, no!' I exhaled in disbelief. 'Let's go outside to play now.'

We ran off into the yard under the fruit trees and

into the street – anywhere possible to avoid doing lessons on my birthday. I knew I would be scolded later on for what I had done, but I would deal with that problem at another time.

My year in Standard Two was the worst in my entire school career. Firstly, many of the students were attacked by an outbreak of malaria. The sanitation department of the Borough of San Fernando mobilised a massive campaign to eradicate mosquitoes. My friends, Dawn and Debbie were ill, and soon after, I, too, became a victim of malaria. I was isolated in a room – left to myself with a mosquito net tucked securely under the mattress all the way around. Three or four times a day, the ghastly quinine liquid was shoved down my throat. Grandpa performed this feat while Aunt Margaret squeezed my nose tightly. On most occasions, the liquid escaped back up my throat and onto the floor, but I soon got another dose and was put to bed again. On mornings when I awoke, the bed linen was soaking wet. I was sweating profusely at one time, and shivering soon after. Aunt Margaret said she feared I would get delirious, so to keep the fever down she used to 'sap' my head with Bay rum and change my clothing several times during the day. It was impossible to refrain from itching when mosquitoes attacked and a plague of eczema ensued. My devoted grandfather painstakingly bathed my arms and legs with a blue medicated soap, which jolted the nerves in my body. As soon as I had recovered, the school routine was quickly imposed once again.

Grandpa was planning to take Gillian and me to spend two weeks in Barataria at Aunt Lily's, when I fell ill again. A typhoid epidemic crippled South Trinidad. Aunt Margaret said the fever was so high that when she touched my neck with the palms of her hand, she could not believe I was so sick. One night, she was speaking to me while I lay in bed. I was wide-awake, but didn't answer her. It was obvious to her that I could not hear her, so she packed a small bag with my clothing and toiletries, lifted me onto her shoulders and took me to the hospital. Two days later, I regained consciousness. It took me a while to realise where I was. The pervading white colour brought me to my senses. I was lying on a small bed, closely sandwiched between two other beds, occupied by two ladies. Their bodies were almost totally draped in white sheets – from neck to toe. The huge room consisted of two rows of beds on opposite sides of the room. The beds seemed to be evenly spaced out, all of our heads lying against the wall, all of our eyes staring across the aisle towards another row of patients in their beds. All the patients took orders from the nurse, who was calling to them to wake up. Some were already awake, sitting up, combing their hair, walking to and from the bathroom area.

'Time to clean up for doctor's rounds,' she called. 'How you feeling dis morning, Savi?' she addressed the lady in the bed opposite to mine. 'You slept well last night?'

'Yes, Nurse; I feel much better. I could go home today?' Savi asked.

'That's not for me to say, my dear. The doctor will be here in the next hour; get yourself cleaned up for his visit and you'll know then. We need beds – a lot of them – so if you're well enough, he'll be happy to discharge you,' she explained. She spun around and looked me squarely in the face. 'And what about you, little miss – how are you this morning?' I slid off the bed trying to stand, but buckled on my way down.

'Oh, no, you don't,' she scolded. 'Get back in bed!'

'Can I use the bathroom, please?' I asked.

'I'll take you – come on.' She helped me off the bed, and wrapped her right arm around my back, supporting my body as I tried to keep up with her pace. In the crook of her left arm, she held toilet paper, soap and toothbrush, which she took from a small cupboard adjacent to my bed. On our return, she reminded us of the doctor's advent and that breakfast would be served afterwards. For lunch, we usually had minced meat and crushed potato or one of several kinds of soup. The best meal was served at teatime – ice cream and cake for the children. Also, it preceded the visiting hour. Friends and relatives were allowed to bring toiletries and other items for patients, but no food. The NO VISITORS sign prohibited them from entering the building. They were allowed to stand before the gate on the steps and converse with nurses on duty, concerning the welfare of their loved ones. 'Jen, your Grandpa was here today,' the nurse informed me. 'He left this story book for you.' *Rulers of the Bible*, the title read – it was a Blackie's Scripture Book. A picture of people from the East adorned the centre of the front cover and inside there were glossy, multi-coloured pages depicting scenes from Bible stories of the Old Testament. Later, I discovered the stories were about Joseph and King Solomon, and Daniel in the lion's den.

'Can I see him for just one minute, please, when he comes again?' I begged her.

'You're not really allowed to. You're not allowed to touch or kiss the visitors. Just say 'hello' and get back inside,' she warned. 'Anyway, if he comes tomorrow, I'll let you see him just for one minute.' Grandpa came and brought oranges, which I was allowed to accept. He was happy to see that I could move about and the nurse, whom he knew, reassured him I was going to be well again in a few weeks. Visitors did not include children, but one afternoon Aunt Margaret and Gillian came to see me.

'You look fine, Jen,' Aunt Margaret commented. 'I brought you two bananas.' She gave them to the nurse, who left and went into the ward.

'What's in the big paper bag, Gillian?' I whispered.

'Come quickly and see,' she beckoned.

There were two beautiful puppies falling over each other as she tilted the bag to show me. 'I want to touch them,' I implored.

'Quick, before Nurse comes back,' she urged.

My two skinny arms slid through the bars of the wooden gate and into the huge bag. The pups were soft and furry and warm. 'Which one do you want?' asked Gillian.

'The black and white one; is it a boy or girl, Gillian?' I asked. I was so excited.

'A boy,' she answered

'Name him Rover. I can't wait to get out of here and hug him tight,' I said with a big grin on my face.

'Here comes the nurse; run back inside,' she warned. 'Don't worry, you'll soon be back home,' she consoled me.

'Bye, Aunt Margaret. Bye, Gillian,' I waved with tears in my eyes.

As the days passed, more and more patients were discharged and fewer patients were admitted. One night, we were kept awake by an old lady who was constantly asking the nurse to go to the bathroom. She prayed and sang and talked to herself. At one point, she was given some water by another patient in the bed next to hers. Then, she settled down and fell asleep. When we awoke the following morning, the nurses on the early shift discovered that she had died and called the wards men to take her body away. Eventually, there were just two children left on the ward – Chandra and myself. Sometimes, we were allowed to play or read together when the nurses were not very busy. Chandra lived in Princes Town.

'My grand-uncle lives in Princes Town,' I told her. 'His name is Uncle Manwar – Manwar Khan, and he has two children, Oli and Hafeeza.'

'Hafeeza? Hafeeza… Khan is your Auntie?' she asked.

'No – Grandpa said she's my cousin – you know her?' I asked curiously.

I was excited to meet someone from Princes Town who actually knew our relatives. Maybe, Grandpa and I could visit Uncle Manwar and Aunt Saleema, and I could spend some time with Hafeeza, and even visit Chandra.

'Hafeeza going to my school, the Presbyterian school; she in one class higher than me,' said Chandra.

'How old are you, Chandra?' I asked. She would be a year or two younger than Hafeeza.

'I have eight years,' she boasted. 'In three years, I will write the Exhibition Examination.'

'And Oli, what school does he go to?' I asked.

'Oh, he going to Naps Boys. I not sure, but he might be in form three,' she said, crossing her lips with her right forefinger as though she was trying to solve a puzzle.

'And Aunt Indrani, you know her too, Chandra? She's Uncle Manwar's sister – Indrani... I don't know her second name – but she was married a long time ago and her husband died. Grandpa said she can read and write just like us – she went to your school. When she started selling chickens and eggs, she kept all her money in a tin under the bed and Uncle Manwar advised her to go to school to learn how to count her money. When she realised how much she had saved, she began banking it.' We both laughed.

'And she still selling chickens and eggs. In Princes Town, everybody call her Ma Bopal. She like children – sometimes she make sweets and give us. But Jen, she really old; she look older than your Grandpa. She not going to live long,' Chandra warned. 'You and your grandpa should go to see her.'

I returned to school having been at the hospital for seven weeks. The following week we were vaccinated for small pox and, soon after, for tuberculosis.

Grandpa had settled into his routine again. He had resumed his post as salesclerk at Uncle Ben's pharmacy, although his working hours were curtailed. He would return home at lunchtime, have a short rest while he read the newspaper for the second time during the day, and then take a late afternoon walk to

Harris Promenade. Twice a week, he gave lessons to two Chinese young men, who had come to Trinidad with their father and couldn't speak a word of English. Their father, Mr Chin, had a laundry on Cipero Street and his second wife was Aunt Margaret's friend. His first wife was still in China. Sometimes, communication became a serious problem between the boys and Grandpa. Gillian and I often wondered if they learnt anything. At one stage, Grandpa attempted to flog them with his leather belt because they were not very alert during the lesson, but he refrained from doing so. After two weeks, we observed that they no longer came to lessons and Grandpa was back to his two good and faithful scholars – Gillian and me.

Reading the newspaper on mornings was an eye-opener. One morning in particular was a gruesome one. A bold headline on the front page of the *Trinidad Guardian* appeared to daunt us – 'Apartheid in South Africa.' We had never seen that word before and would be in grave danger if we couldn't find the meaning – so we went to get the dictionary to help us. Gillian, four years my senior, was better at English than I was – so she flicked through the pages eagerly, while I spelt out the word for her. She didn't find the meaning. Her father, who always had a stack of library books in his room, kept a dictionary on his bureau, so she brought out that one as well. We both searched through its pages laboriously.

'Jen, Gillian,' Grandpa called as we lay, sprawled on the dining room floor behind the large table. He was getting impatient. 'What's the matter with you two? All you need to do is follow the alphabet!' he shouted.

'Hurry, Gillian – I don't want to feel that belt so early in the morning,' I said apprehensively.

'It's not here, Jen – there's no word like that in the dictionary,' she moaned. We both looked at the relevant page and ran our forefingers down the row of words beginning with 'ap.'

'Come on, children,' Grandpa called again. Defeated, we walked slowly towards him, each of us holding an open book, pressed against our bodies. Gillian, the more courageous, addressed him. 'It's not in the dictionary, Grandpa. Jen and I looked through both dictionaries and we can't find the meaning.'

He was beginning to get annoyed, 'That's impossible. You two are growing more stupid, instead of becoming more intelligent – too much play in your heads.' I thought we were about to receive a thrashing, when he said to Gillian, 'Give me that book. I'll find it myself.'

We stood behind him, peering through the bifocal lenses of his spectacles, while he searched through the page with his forefinger, the same way we had done. Gillian wanted to tilt the rocking chair backwards as she rested her foot on the curved tip of the rocker, but changed her mind as Grandpa stood up. He went to the dining room cupboard, took out a magnifying glass and rested the dictionary on the table.

'I can't seem to find that word here,' he admitted, 'in either of the dictionaries. Get your exercise books, children, and write down that word. You'll have to go to the library to find the meaning,' he concluded.

I asked Grandpa if we could go to Princes Town to see Uncle Manwar and his children. But before he could decide on a day during the Easter vacation, Aunt Indrani fell ill and was taken to San Fernando hospital. Children were not allowed into the wards, so Gillian and I couldn't see her. We met Uncle Manwar on the hospital compound and Grandpa said something to him about Aunt Indrani making a will, before she got worse. Later that day, they both went to a lawyer on Irving Street and Aunt Indrani died that same week. Grandpa attended the funeral in Princes Town and after that Oli, Uncle Manwar's son, came to see us sometimes after school.

Gillian was growing into a big girl – she was fourteen and attending Naparima Girls' High School. Grandpa couldn't really help her much, now that she was studying Latin and French and Biology. But he insisted that Arithmetic didn't change and surprisingly, he could do the sums in her arithmetic text book. He often urged me to try to do some of those sums. I thought the idea was too ambitious, although I tried sometimes. We were preoccupied with voluntarily studying, now that we were growing up. I would soon be writing the Exhibition Examination, an entrance examination to Secondary school. However, the effort to concentrate was soon to be broken by a domestic crisis involving Aunt Margaret.

One night after Grandpa, Gillian and I had read the usual three chapters from the Bible and said our prayers, we closed all the windows and doors in the living and dining rooms, and went upstairs to bed. Gillian and I usually slept in Aunt Rose's old room, but when Aunt Margaret came home early I slept with her, and Gillian stayed downstairs with her parents.

Aunt Margaret was away from home very often and Grandpa had spoken to her about coming in late at night. Grandpa occupied the bedroom nearest the upstairs back door, which he locked promptly at nine o'clock – unless an unusual circumstance arose. We had just switched off the bedroom light and settled into bed, when we heard noises beneath us in the dining room. 'What's that?' I asked Gillian.

'Sounds like Aunt Margaret, closing the door,' she replied.

'You think Grandpa heard her?' I asked again.

'I doubt that,' she said. 'He's getting deaf these days. She had better keep quiet before Grandpa hears something; he's not sleeping,' I told her. 'He's waiting to see what time she'll come home tonight.'

But, Grandpa didn't just lie still in his bed. We heard him unlock the back door, then switch on the light over the back stairs. Clip, clap, went his alpagatas as he stepped down briskly. Gillian and I got out of bed, and wormed our way to the back door entrance to hear what was happening. As he unlocked the door downstairs, went in and switched on the light, Gillian and I slid down the banister and stepped quietly along the side entrance to the dining room. The front door was wide open. Aunt Margaret had just entered through the doorway.

An argument ensued between Grandpa and Aunt Margaret. We listened to Grandpa threaten Aunt Margaret and say that, if she couldn't behave like decent people, she may as well pack her things and find somewhere else to live. The argument developed into an angry outburst by both parties. Grandpa raised his hand high up above his head and Aunt Margaret screamed, 'Don't hit me, Pa. I'm too old for that!'

'Then make this the last day you bring your worthlessness to this house, and embarrass me,' he shouted at her. Later that day, we saw two strong men take all of Aunt Margaret's furniture from her room to the yard. They left everything exposed to the elements. In the afternoon, Aunt Margaret said she was going to stay at a friend's, but she would be back for me the next day. 'Don't tell Grandpa or Gillian,' she warned. 'You must keep this a secret between us.'

Aunt Margaret came with a truck and took her furniture, and our clothes and me to her friend's house – Aunt Dora's, who managed a steam laundry owned by Mr Chin. We stayed at Aunt Dora's for six months, then Aunt Margaret said she was going to build a new house on a piece of land, which Grandma had left her. Three old wooden houses sat on the land and she had rented them to other people for six years since Grandma's death. It was situated on Gordon Street and I was happy about that because I could visit Grandpa everyday and still live with Aunt Margaret.

After Aunt Margaret and I moved into her new house, I went to see Grandpa again. He had sold most of the bedroom furniture from upstairs and moved downstairs to live. He said the doctor advised him that climbing the steps was not the best thing for his heart, so he had decided to rent upstairs to some people he knew at church. Aunt Margaret said I might as well stay with her because Grandpa didn't have enough room for me and soon I would need my own room as I was growing into a big girl. So I stayed with Aunt

Margaret and every evening, I went to sleep with Grandpa, and every morning, I trekked up the big hill back to Aunt Margaret's to get dressed for school.

Grandpa was definitely becoming less active and now walked fairly slowly on his way to the promenade. He spent more time at home and less on the road. On mornings after he had read the newspaper, he had breakfast and a bath, got dressed and left home at about ten o'clock for his usual walk. When he reached the promenade, he took a rest and then proceeded towards the library, on to Mucurapo Street to Uncle Ben's pharmacy, where he chatted with the customers, especially those who spoke Hindi. I never understood their conversation except odd words and phrases, which Grandpa had taught Gillian and me at home. Aunt Margaret said he had tried to teach her Hindi too, but her brain just couldn't learn the language. Often, it was difficult for the Hindi speakers to express themselves in English and they were reluctant to visit an unfamiliar doctor or dentist in the town. So, Uncle Ben was called upon to suggest what medication they should purchase for their ailments. Sometimes, a request was made for him to extract a tooth. This situation prompted Grandpa and Uncle Ben to persuade our island scholar, his son Omar, to study medicine. It was Grandpa's dream come true – a unique scholastic achievement. So Grandpa usually returned home at lunchtime, after having stopped at the market, bought his bananas and chatted some more with his friends, some of whom were market vendors.

Myrtle no longer worked at the family house, so Aunt Annette, Gillian's mother, cooked and

Miss Abraham, an elderly lady from our church, did Grandpa's laundry. Every Saturday afternoon, I spent several hours keeping him company. We sat on the benches at the promenade and talked, listened to the police band play in the bandstand and bought hot peanuts from the vendors at the library corner. Sometimes, we stood before Mahatma Gandhi's statue and once again, Grandpa would relate Gandhi's unflinching determination towards gaining independence for India. There was something about this hero that mesmerised my grandfather. He could never just walk past the statue – he always bowed to it. He revealed a strange fascination for a man with whom he seemed to share an affinity – steadfast yet peaceful, ambitious yet humble, with a deep-seated concern for others amid his own difficulties.

In Standard Four, we worked tirelessly, making notes in Geography, Civics and Hygiene, solving arithmetic problems and absorbing all the rules in Nestfield's Grammar. My teacher occasionally visited me at home to discuss problems he thought I might have. I guess he felt comfortable doing so since he knew my family and lived in San Fernando. Finally, the dreaded day arrived when I went to the Roman Catholic Boys' School to write the Exhibition Examination. Grandpa sat all day on the promenade until the examination was over. Unfortunately, I did not win a scholarship and went on to write the entrance examination to Naparima Girls'. At last, I entered secondary school – to Grandpa's relief and Aunt Margaret's delight.

My first year in high school was eventful, not only

for me, but for San Fernando and Trinidad as a whole. Everybody talked about the forthcoming elections. Grandpa said that finally poor people would be able to vote and elect their own representatives in the government. There was a surge of political meetings on the Harris Promenade and Irving Street. The *Trinidad Guardian* printed photographs of the 1956 election candidates. There was a new party leader, Dr Eric Williams, who addressed the San Fernando public at Harris Promenade. He was an eloquent speaker and had a photographic memory for biblical quotations and figures. Several motorcades broke the silence of our sleepy town as we lined the streets to wave and shout to familiar party supporters, who drove past in cars and soft drink trucks. A jubilant political party supporter called out to Grandpa and admonished him to 'Vote for Roy', but I knew he was impressed with the slate of candidates from the opposing party – whose motto, 'Interracial Solidarity' won a majority of elected seats. When Grandpa read the results in the newspaper that morning, he boasted about his red-stained forefinger which had kept him company for a full week. I was happy to see him engrossed in the political activity of the country. Sometimes, he cancelled his morning walk to follow the post-election developments in the newspaper, and sometimes, he would stop at Mr Juman's on Keate Street to discuss the latest events and never reached the promenade. It was a welcome sight to see him brimming over with excitement in his old age after a long spell of retirement hibernation.

One evening after dinner, Gillian and I were

studying for our term examinations and I fell asleep with my head on the table. I was awakened by Grandpa's voice: 'You haven't done any work tonight, Jen. You're wasting the electricity – go to bed and I'll wake you early in the morning.'

When I awoke the following morning, my eyes were red and puffy. I couldn't understand why I was having difficulty reading what was written on the blackboard at school. When I brought home the school report, Aunt Margaret was horrified.

'You've never placed this low in class,' she commented, 'something must be wrong.'

Grandpa voiced the same sentiments and I confessed to him that I couldn't see what was written on the blackboard. He made an appointment with an eye specialist in Port of Spain who had been his student at Vistabella Presbyterian School twenty years ago. For a moment, I thought I might be sick and would need to be hospitalised again. The doctor took a urine sample, which Grandpa explained was relevant since both my grandparents had diabetes. Then he tested my eyes and said I needed spectacles because I was short-sighted. That was a historical event in my family because Aunt Margaret said I was the first to have an eye problem at such an early age. In one week, we returned to have my glasses fitted, 'a guarantee of good results,' Grandpa threatened.

One Sunday morning, I waited for my grandfather who usually passed Aunt Margaret's house on the way to church. It was nine-thirty and we had very little time to get to church before the service started at ten o'clock. I ran down the front steps and looked South along the street. There was no sign of him.

'Something's happened,' Aunt Margaret said. 'The world must be coming to an end, or his name is not Clarence Stephen Sanowar. Go down and meet him, Jen – maybe he's just late today.'

But I knew he wasn't just late – he was never late. His routine was like clockwork. Tears filled my eyes as I hurried along, nervously, towards the house. When I got there, he was sitting in his rocking chair, picking out notes to a hymn from his Book of Praise.

'Good morning, Grandpa,' I greeted him and kissed him on his forehead – the safest part of his face, I thought, to avoid colliding with his spectacles.

'Good morning, Beti,' he replied, as he continued to sing a broken tune.

'Aren't we going to church this morning, Grandpa?' I was totally confounded.

'Church? Not this morning, Beti; I woke up late and couldn't get dressed in time – so we'll go next Sunday – all right? Oh! You're dressed up and ready for church – why don't you go ahead, then?' he suggested.

But I didn't want to go without him. Besides, I wanted to find out the story behind his strange behaviour that morning. I went to the kitchen, and met Aunt Annette and Gillian washing the breakfast dishes and tidying the kitchen.

'Good morning, Auntie. Hi Gillian! What happened to Grandpa this morning?' I asked.

'Didn't he tell you?' Gillian faced me squarely, arms akimbo.

'Tell me what?' I asked blankly.

Aunt Annette explained. 'He was going to the bathroom this morning and fell on the step, and bruised himself. He couldn't get up, so Gillian and I helped him up and put him back to bed. He had breakfast, then went to his rocker and has been singing from his hymn book ever since.'

When I related to Aunt Margaret what had happened, she said that as soon as she was finished preparing lunch, she would go to see him. That afternoon it was impossible to contact a doctor privately, so Aunt Margaret decided to telephone Uncle Andrew, Aunt Lily's husband, for help. His nephew, a young medical practitioner, lived in Medical Quarters and worked at the San Fernando Colonial Hospital. Aunt Margaret said it would be better for Grandpa if a doctor could visit him at home quietly, then advise the family whether he should be taken to the hospital or remain at home. Usually, on Sunday evenings, I stayed with Aunt Margaret. But under the circumstances, she felt I should keep Grandpa's company in case he fell ill during the night. Dawn and Debbie's great aunt, Tantie, suspecting that something was wrong as Aunt Margaret seldom visited the family house, asked if everything was okay. Aunt Margaret replied, 'Pa just fell, Tantie; the doctor will come in the morning, and then I'll let you know if it's serious or not.'

'Your Pa needs a rest, child. From the time I know him, he's been trudging up and down this road. Maybe I should go over and give him a little rub down this evening,' she suggested.

We smiled at the idea. 'That's okay, Tantie,' Aunt

Margaret assured her. 'You know Pa; he's so very independent, he's behaving as though nothing happened.'

'He's a proud man, child, but at his age he needs care and attention and company. You coming back later, Jen – to stay with Grandpa?' she called to me.

'Yes, Tantie,' I answered.

Aunt Margaret and I chuckled at the idea of Tantie rubbing down Grandpa. She was a tiny character, fragile in appearance, and usually gripped the banister of the staircase with all her might because she couldn't see two steps in front of her. Besides, neither Aunt Margaret nor I could remember ever getting that close to Grandpa, much less to remove his clothes and rub him down!

That night, for the first time ever, my grandfather talked in his sleep and woke up very early to sit in his rocking chair. Also for the first time ever, he asked me to get the newspaper on the front step and his hymn book from his chest of drawers.

Dr Perelli came at seven in the morning. He told Aunt Annette that Grandpa needed to stay in bed for most of the day. He could have his meals at the table, but should not go to the bathroom and so, someone would have to 'sponge' him in bed. He had had a heart attack, but rest and quiet were the best medication he could offer at that time. He assured her that he would be back in the evening at about seven o'clock. Grandpa stayed in bed for four days. Aunt Margaret 'sponged' him after breakfast and everyday, she prepared a special soup for his lunch. When Dr Perelli examined him on the fifth day, he called the ambulance to have him taken to the hospital.

One afternoon, on our way to visit him, I asked Aunt Margaret Grandpa's age.

'Eighty-six,' she replied.

'When was he eighty-six? I can't remember him celebrating his birthday,' I said.

'That's because he has never celebrated his birthday. He always insisted he was born in May, but doesn't know the exact date. Before Aunt Rose went to Canada, he used to participate in her birthday activities on the twelfth of May, but after that he never bothered,' she explained.

'Auntie Margaret, can I make a cake for Grandpa?' I asked.

'Of course,' she answered. 'But, remember, he'll only be able to eat a slice or two because he's diabetic.'

Aunt Margaret visited Grandpa twice everyday. In the mornings, she took him clean clothing and towels, and collected his soiled clothing. On afternoons, we both went to the hospital, and she took toiletries or fruit or any item the nurse had requested for him. There was always a stream of visitors around his bed – teachers, students, church members, neighbours, relatives and friends. Sometimes, the nurse would ask the visitors to leave if they overstayed their visiting time. On weekends, the ward was particularly crowded. Aunt Margaret and I didn't take foodstuff at the weekend because Grandpa's friends from the country areas brought him oranges, bananas and grapefruits. When they made him talk too much, the nurse asked them to leave.

On the second Friday of his confinement, Grandpa asked Aunt Margaret to telephone Aunt Lily and Uncle

Andrew. He wanted to speak to them urgently. They came to San Fernando on the following Sunday, had lunch with us, and then we all went to the hospital in their blue Opel. Aunt Margaret and I waited in the front gallery to give them some privacy.

The following morning, Aunt Margaret decided she would wait to see Dr Perelli as he made his ward rounds. She was becoming very anxious about Grandpa's condition, and the fact that there was no dialogue concerning his discharge from hospital. That morning luck was on our side. The staff nurse said that Dr Perelli would be late, so after breakfast was served, we were allowed to stay with Grandpa for a while.

'How're you feeling this morning, Pa?' Aunt Margaret asked him.

'Oh, Beti, I feel a little tired; I didn't sleep too well last night. The hospital bed feels strange and I couldn't get up and sit in my rocker and sing the way I can at home,' he complained.

'I will ask the nurse if you could sit out in the front gallery after lunch, and I can bring two cushions for you,' Aunt Margaret suggested, but he seemed not to have heard her.

'How you managing, child – with the loan and Jen and yourself?' he sounded not just concerned, but a bit worried about her.

'Oh, Pa, don't think about that now. I asked Ben to rent a building he owns on the Coffee, and next month, I'm going to start a food business,' she assured him.

'What do you know about running a business?' he voiced surprise. 'And how are you so sure about this venture?'

'Pa, that is a busy area; there are two car sale companies, a supermarket, and a mechanic repair shop. Coffee Street has a lot of business places. People want lunch to eat everyday, especially the men. At first, I can sell snacks and sandwiches. I got a lady to make *roti* already. And if sales pick up later on, I will cook lunch – and Pa, that is where I can make a profit.'

'And who is going to help you with all the heavy work?' he asked.

'Myrtle's son will be working with me, and if I need her, Myrtle said she can help too,' Aunt Margaret replied.

Grandpa raised his eyebrows, 'Makes some sense to me – but you must be careful, Beti, for your own safety and protection. You chose hard work and I'm glad to hear you doing something to help yourself. I know you don't have much money so I have this for you – to help a little. Use it wisely. It took a long time to save it.' He handed her a cheque.

'One thousand dollars!' she exclaimed.

'Now, don't let everybody hear my business,' he scolded her. 'Put it in the bank until you need it.'

On the last day we visited Grandpa, we met Uncle Manwar and his son, Oli. Uncle was relating his son's history at Naparima College since he had passed his examinations, and was now employed as a clerk at the Town Hall. Uncle Manwar was excited about Oli's accomplishments.

'And Bhai, Oli take after yuh,' he said to Grandpa, and quickly turning to Oli, he continued, 'yuh take after yuh *Chacha*, boy.' He looked at Grandpa again and said, 'Bhai, he have a real good head for

Mat'ematics. It was his bes' subject right t'rough College, Bhai.'

Grandpa had said that Uncle was only a few years younger than he, but he was a lively old man. He was tall and slim, his hair now greying with a slight curl here and there. He wore a white *kurta* and trousers with sandals whenever he came to San Fernando.

Oli was twenty-one; he resembled Uncle Manwar in appearance, but his manner was more like Grandpa's. He had been working at the Town Hall for six months.

'And what kind of work are you doing at the Town Hall, Oli?' Grandpa asked him.

'I'm working in the town clerk's office, Uncle,' he replied proudly. 'I'm learning a great deal about San Fernando.' Grandpa was impressed.

'A good position – you will meet important people and this can create opportunities for you. Do your work well, son; you're still young and later on, if you want to improve yourself in a chosen field of study, you'll be able to get good advice from your superiors.'

'Uncle, I think, in a few years' time, I want to join the new political party. For the first time in Trinidad, a party leader is encouraging all people to get together and work for the benefit of the country. We never heard about that before; and there's even talk about independence. What does that mean for us, Uncle?' Oli asked Grandpa.

Grandpa smiled. It was a difficult question. He had neither the energy nor the understanding of politics to answer Oli honestly. 'You will just have to wait and see, Beta, and seize the opportunity as it comes along. I must say you've done well for yourself – and don't forget your Baap here, who didn't have the opportunity you had. We tried our best, and we are old now. Our children must continue to provide better conditions for their children. Your Baap and I – our struggle is over. We must rest now.'

'Bhai,' said Uncle Manwar, as he embraced Grandpa, 'de struggle put all o' we in a better position; it worth every minute o' it.'

Aunt Margaret and I hugged Grandpa and kissed him goodbye. Uncle Manwar and Oli walked through the hospital compound with us, then proceeded to the train station near the Wharf.

As we passed through the hospital gateway and were about to cross the street, we heard someone behind us calling, 'Stop, Miss Margaret, stop!'

It was a hospital wards man. As he gasped for breath, he held Aunt Margaret's hands in his and stammered, 'Miss Mar-garet – ah so sorry, Miss Margaret. Yuh Pa jus' pass away – de doctor say was a heart attack.'

Aunt Margaret's screams attracted a small crowd. She retreated towards the gateway and reached out with both hands to clutch the nearby lamppost for support. The wards man helped her to sit on an embankment. She held her face in her open palms as the tears streamed through her fingers. I did not know what to say or do. The people began to move away. Then, she raised her head and realised we were the only two people left there. As I sat close to her, she encircled my body with her right arm.

'Oh Jen,' she said to me, 'what are we going to do

now? I am not going back in there. I want to remember Pa how I last saw him.' She rose slowly off the embankment, took up her handbag, held my hand and we walked home in silence.

Glossary

Baap	father
baigan	eggplant, melongene
Beti	young girl
beta	young boy
bhagi	spinach
Bhai	big brother
bhowji	sister-in-law
carat house	house covered with large carat or palm leaves
chewry	necklace
chacha	uncle
cocoyea broom	broom made from the rib of coconut palm leaves
Divali	Hindu celebration – festival of lights
dyahs	small, clay vessels, in which oil is put and used in Hindu celebrations
Eid	Muslim Holy Day
Hindi	one of the official languages of India
Hindustani	a dialect of Hindi
Hosay	Muslim celebration
imam	Muslim priest
kurta	long shirt worn over trousers
Nana	grandfather

ohrni	short veil
pundit	Hindu priest
pera	low stool
pommerac	rose apple
pommecythere	golden apple
Sahib	Sir, name used to address someone in authority
sirdar	supervisor, overseer
sawine	a spiced, milk-based dessert served at Eid celebrations
tadjah	ornate structures built to commemorate Hosay
TGIT	Trinidad Girls in Training

Sterling Currency

One pound = $4.80
One dollar = 4s 2d
One pound = 20s
One penny = 4 farthings

Lightning Source UK Ltd.
Milton Keynes UK
UKOW05f0231300617
304364UK00001B/8/P